Amarugia

(Am-a-ROO-GEE)

Robert L. "Bob" Gross

First Printing

Published by
Southern Lion Books
Historical Publications
1280 Westminster Way
Madison, Georgia 30650

southernlionbooks.com

Manufactured in the United States of America.

Library of Congress Control Number: 2008943687

ISBN: 978-0-9794203-9-9

The paper in this book meets the guidelines for permanence and durability of the Committee on Production Guidelines for Book Longevity of the Council on Library Resources.

Front Cover Artwork by Stan Himes
Back Cover Photo by Donald Lewis Osborn

Acknowledgments

I acknowledge my appreciation to Donald Lewis Osborn and his book, *Tales of the Amarugia Highlands of Cass County, Missouri* and for other assistance he has given. Thanks to Jim Arnold for his help when we revisited the sites upon which this novel is based. Also, thanks to the personnel of the Cass County Public Library and the Cass County Historical Society in Harrisonville, Missouri.

I am grateful for Sally Lee's writing class and the Word-Smiths.Ink class at the FiftyForward Martin Center in Brentwood, Tennessee. I am grateful to Stan Hime for his drawings and sketches. I especially thank Sheri Swanson for editing this novel and Brenda Brothers for typesetting. Additionally, I appreciate my computer technician, Frank Leake; and thank you, Hank Segars, Managing Editor of Southern Lion Books, Inc.

Donald Lewis Osborn holding a copy of his book,
Tales of the Amarugia Highlands of Cass County, Missouri.

Introduction

While the story you're about to read is fiction, The Kingdom of Amarugia really did/does exist. It is an area of approximately 20 square miles located in Cass County, Missouri, approximately 50 miles south of Kansas City. Around 1830 the Hudson Bay Fur Company may have established a fur trading post in this area. A man by the name of Basy Owens, an agent of the Hudson Bay Fur Company supposedly explored and colonized the area around 1830. Several families from eastern Kentucky, eastern Tennessee, and western Virginia, moved here. These folks preferred to live in the hilly part of the area. Also, persons moved to this part of Missouri from Ohio, Indiana, and Illinois, but they preferred to live in the prairie area just south of the Amarugia Highlands. To have peace and harmony it was thought a government was necessary. A council was convened and an absolute monarchy was established with Basy Owens as the head of the Kingdom.

The early settlers discovered that fur was not as plentiful as they first thought. There were also civil disagreements. There was an invasion by the tribes from the prairie at one time. It is said they captured the King and held him for ransom for several years. The Kingdom refused to pay a ransom for his return and disease caused the King's death. Owens II proclaimed himself as King and led the people to pursue agriculture. Petty warfare took place from time to time between Amarugia and the farmers of the Prairie.

During the mid 1800s, there was much looting and burning between the Union and Confederate troops in the area. On August 21, 1863, a man by the name of William Quantrill led a group of men to burn Lawrence, Kansas, and executed 150 men. In response, Union General Thomas Ewing issued Order Number 11.

All civilians in Jackson, Cass, Bates, and northern Vernon County had 15 days to leave and move. The countryside, including all fields, homes, barns and goods was burned to establish a neutral zone where the guerrillas (Quantrill's men) could not hide. The area became known as the Burnt District. Only the chimneys of the cabins remained. They were called "Jennison's Tombstones" after the Kansas Jayhawks leader "Doc" Jennison whose troops did much of the burning and looting. The population of Cass County fell from 10,000 to 600. Only 30 percent of its residents returned after the war.

This novel is a fiction story about two boys who grew up there around 1910-1911. During this time a man by the name of David W. Wilson had taken the title of King of Amarugia as documented by the history book entitled *Tales of the Amarugia Highlands of Cass County, Missouri* by Donald Lewis Osborn. King David Wilson ruled for 18 years, from 1895 to 1913. The setting for this novel is in the year 1910.

The author, Robert L. "Bob" Gross, grew up on an 80-acre farm at the edge of Amarugia from 1931 to 1944, except for the first three grades of school. He lived with his grandparents in Archie, Missouri, during those three years. His family had a small dairy and raised mules for sale. Many of the experiences in the novel are either his or those people he knew.

This log cabin was one of the few structures in Cass County
to survive the Kansas-Missouri Border War, the Civil War,
and Order No. 11, in the "Burnt District". It was reconstructed by the
Cass County Historical Society on its present site at
400 East Mechanic Street, Harrisonville, Missouri.

Table of Contents

SPRING—1910

SUMMER—1910

Fall—1910

WINTER—1910

Amarugia

(Am-a-ROO-GEE)

SPRING—1910

Chapter 1—Moving Day

The clouds moved in fast. The wind shook and twisted the trees along the side of the road. A bolt of lightning struck and split a tall hedge tree wide open just to the right of the wagon. The smell of burnt wood filled the air and the blinding flash and crackle spooked the horses who reared up, whinnying as they lunged to the left. Both dogs howled as the noise hurt their ears, and Betty and her mother, Mae, screamed from the buggy following behind them.

Tim held his breath as he watched his father, B.J., keep control of the team, quieting Bell and Blaze with firm commands. Unfortunately, he couldn't avoid the rut that sent the right front wheel flying and the side of the wagon crashing to the ground. As the rain came down in gully-gutting gushes, Tim jumped from his seat, and ran to his mother and sister shuddering in the buggy which was following right behind. "Are you O.K.?" they asked each other, almost in unison. Apparently only their nerves were jangled.

"Mae, hold the bridles so these horses will calm down until we get this wheel back on the wagon." Turning back, he shouted over the thunder and rain, "Tim, you and Betty come on over and help me unload the tools and heavier things. We need to take some weight off this right side." By the time they finished, the sun had replaced the thunderheads, and a beautiful rainbow stretched across the Eastern sky.

"Now there. See. Storm's passed and we're just fine. Tim, give me a hand over here. Betty-Boo, bring me that roll of bailing wire, please. Now, on three, Tim and I are going to lift, and you're going to slide that wheel right back on its axle. Got it?" Betty took hold of the wheel.

"Just like this?"

She gingerly put it back on the axle and Mr. Smith wound the wire tightly around the end of the axle to prevent another lost wheel. As they reloaded the wagon, he told the children more about their new home.

"I know it's less than ten miles from our house in Archie, but life on the farm will require some adjustment...."

"Daddy? Are all the storms out this way so big?"

"Well, Betty-Boo, sometimes smaller, sometimes bigger. We won't have as many trees out on those eighty acres to protect us, so Grandpa and I built a storm cellar. Next time one of these blows over from Kansas, we'll hide out in it until the storm passes."

"Is it dark? And smelly? Are there snakes in it? Sounds like it may be scarier than the storm!"

Mrs. Smith chuckled. "No, sweetheart, we'll take a lantern or two with us when we go. And it's not just for storms, since it'll be nice and cool below ground, we'll use it to store all those vegetables we'll be canning, our milk, and our butter. So really, it'll be like a part of the house."

Relieved, Betty started firing off questions in her usual fashion. "What else will we have on the farm? Will we have different chores? Will I get my own horse? Do I still have to go to school? How will I make friends? Can I stay up late?" Betty, even at 13, never seemed to run out of questions.

Mr. and Mrs. Smith exchanged a smile as Tim, feeling quite grown up after helping hold up the wagon, rolled his twelve-year-old eyes.

"Well, we'll have a garden—a big one—with corn and strawberries, and watermelons," stated Mrs. Smith, naming three of her daughter's favorite foods. "Grandpa's planted apple and cherry trees so we'll have plenty for canning and pies and jams and for selling. Then, of course, we'll have all sorts of animals, besides our mules and horses, and our dogs, Jack and Pumpkin. We'll have cows and chickens...."

Cass County, Missouri, Map

Location in the state of Missouri

Missouri's location in the USA

Statistics

Founded: 1835
Seat: Harrisonville
Population: (2000) 82,092
Density 45/km²

Area
  Total 1,820 km² (703 mi²)
  Land 1,810 km² (699 mi²)
  Water 10 km² (4 mi²), 0.52%

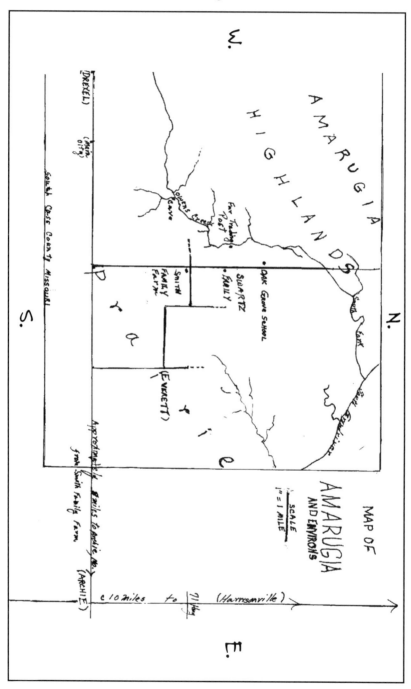

Betty asked, "I love chickens! May I feed them and gather their eggs, and watch their chicks?"

"Of course you may, but you'll have to watch out for the roosters—they don't like it if they think their hens are in danger. We'll have animals on the farm that can kick you, step on you, butt you with their heads, scare you, bite you, poop and pee on you, and no telling what else. Some of them will run at you; others will run from you when you want them to come to you, but most of the time you will find them to be very loving; and each animal has his own personality."

Mr. Smith continued, "However, try not to get too attached to the animals we'll be raising for food; remember—we get our meat from our farm animals and this means, when the time comes, we'll need to kill, dress, and cook them for breakfast, dinner, or supper." Tim and Betty's eyes widened. They hadn't thought of that.

"You'll also have to watch out for Captain Midnight," interrupted Tim, trying to sound stern. "Papa says he'll chase you if you tease him, or if you mess with his cows or their calves."

"Who in the world is Captain Midnight?" Betty asked.

"Our new Angus bull." Tim didn't quite know what the Angus part meant, but he did know that keeping him in the pasture kept the cattle rustlers away and that his daddy and grandfather had put the bull's head into a stall and put a big brass ring in his nose.

"Oh, something else that's very important for us to remember: we can't play with the baby piglets—we'll make the mama sow mad and she'll come after us and try to bite or gore us with her tusks to protect her babies."

Mr. Smith noticed how well the boy had been listening before the storm and smiled to himself. Betty continued peppering her mother with questions. "What about school, Mama? And friends? And...."

"Gracious child, one question at a time! School. You and your brother will most definitely attend Oak Grove School, which, before you ask, is a mile and a half up the road from our house, so you'll make friends there and I suspect, in 4-H Club, if that's something you decide you'd like to do."

Turning to Tim, she told them more. "There are a couple of churches and a grocery store in Everett, about two miles from our house. When we get all the farm work caught up, we'll probably start attending one of those churches. And Tim, I know you'll be excited to know that I've heard that there're several good places to fish in Amarugia."

"I'm really anxious to get started," Tim said. "It sure sounds like there will be lots to see and do on our farm."

Pointing at the rainbow, Tim continued, "You know, Grandma Smith says that the Bible says that the rainbow is a sign from God that the whole world will never be destroyed again by a flood like it was when Noah lived."

"Let's hope not! We've come through our first big encounter with the weather. The rain is a blessing, but the wind and lightning can be a curse," Mr. Smith reminded them, "Well, we can't get there till we get started. Tim, why don't you take the buggy with Betty; and Mae, Honey, you ride up here with me in the wagon the rest of the way."

They had to get to the farm as soon as possible because Grandpa's renters were moving to Harrisonville, and the Smiths would have to perform the evening chores: milk the cows, slop the hogs, and check for any eggs among the hens.

"The dogs can ride in the buggy. Keep them on their leashes so they won't jump off," Mr. Smith suggested. "And Tim?"

"Yes Sir?"

"The roads are very slick so mind the ruts. We'll have to travel slower." The young horses and the mule were also anxious to get started again.

Before the move, Mr. Smith had worked in his father-in-law's hardware store in Adrian, Missouri, six miles—or two hours each way—from the family home in Archie, but his wages weren't enough to support a family of four. Hoping to make a better life for the family, he and his wife planned to work his father's farm and raise a big garden and truck patch, sell milk and cream, have all the fruits and vegetables they needed during the growing season, and can enough fruits and vegetables to last through the winter months. He also planned to raise mules, break them to work in the harness, and then sell them as well-trained animals ready to work in the fields.

As they caravanned to the farm, they encountered the cooing of turtle doves, the chirping of cardinals, and the caws of crows in the distance. As rabbits ran across the road or turtledoves erupted from their nests, the dogs would bark and, at first, the horses would shy, but soon the family animals adjusted to the new wild life around them.

Having devoured his sandwich, Tim munched on an apple, feeling very grown up on what seemed like the adventure of a lifetime. He could tell Betty thought so too. His dad just wanted the best for his family, and while Tim didn't know it, his mom probably felt the most nervous of them all, having never lived on a farm before now. He turned to his sister beside him.

"Last night I overheard Mom praying for us and our trip."

"During this storm today I think all of us got caught up on our praying. I know I did. That was scary!"

"That storm made me realize that out here in the country we need to pay more attention to the weather. Rains are important for good crops, but sometimes they scare the holy bejabers out of a guy. I'm sure glad mom prayed for us."

The sun continued to dry the road and by the time another wagon or two happened by, they managed to pass without sliding into the ditch.

Finally, around four in the afternoon, they arrived at the farmhouse. What a feeling of excitement!

"Look Tim; there are the hens and roosters and even a turkey gobbler!"

"I can see a little pond which is close to the barn. I wonder if it has fish in it."

"We'll sure have a lot of questions for Dad because he is the only one who has ever lived on a farm."

Mrs. Smith's heart beat fast. She had never had a house of her own. It was smaller than the two-story tile house they'd shared with Grandpa and Grandma Smith in Archie, but it was large enough for the four of them. Mr. Smith had told her that she would be "Queen of the House" and he would be "King of the Farm" and he added that together they would be "King and Queen" of everything else. *"It will certainly be a great adventure for our entire family!"* she thought.

Mr. Smith and Tim unhitched the horses and mule, gave them a drink in the little pond, and hung up the harnesses on hooks in the barn. Tim's dad showed him where to find the feed. After giving the work horses a generous helping of oats and corn and some hay—a chore that hereafter would belong to Tim—they set about unloading the tools and furniture. In the meantime, the girls took the food and cooking utensils to the kitchen and the linens to the bedrooms. Then they gathered around the kitchen table to read the note left by the Monroes,

> *Welcome home Smith family! We hope you had an easy trip from Archie. We know you'll have plenty to do, so John made sure you had enough wood to get your supper made.*
>
> *Now about the cows. The brown and white cow may try to step into the bucket as you milk her, so be on your guard. The solid brown one will try to be the first one to come in the door of the milk shed, so you might as well milk her first. There is plenty of ice in the cellar to keep the milk cool and fresh. You may want to bring up some of the ice and put it in the ice box in the kitchen. We've left the piano for you.*
>
> *We hope you'll be as happy here as we were. Regards to Mr. & Mrs. Smith Sr.*
>
> *God Bless,*
> *The Monroes*

Betty glanced out the back porch door and noticed how happily Jack and Pumpkin explored their new home; even if at first the squawking chickens and guinea hens startled them. Her mother's voice brought her back from her thoughts about the dogs.

"We don't have much money. Betty, you'll need to go see how many eggs the hens have laid. Your dad told me we should find several eggs by this time of day. We should be able to sell most of them at the Everett store and get some of the things on our grocery list, but for now, let's get supper started." Betty started out the door.

"Oh, and on your way back from the hen house, would you please stop by the garden and look for something which would make a salad? Thanks, Sweetheart." Mrs. Smith added.

When she came back, Betty announced, "I found some lettuce, radishes, and onions."

"There is some cured ham we brought with us to go with the salad," added Mrs. Smith.

While the girls acquainted themselves with the new kitchen, the boys headed out to the barn. Tim's father had warned him that it might take a little longer to do the milking after a big rain.

"I hope we can build a modern dairy barn with a concrete floor sometime in the future," Mr. Smith said as they headed for the milk barn, a lean-to shed with a dirt floor attached to the big barn.

"But we will just have to take things one step at a time. If this mud gets much deeper we'll have to wash the udders of the cows with a damp cloth before we milk them." Tim took Jack, the collie, and started teaching him how to drive the cows from the pasture to the milking shed.

Brownie and the other cows were soon in their stalls munching feed. Tim and his dad each took one of the milking stools and sat while they milked the cows from the right hand side. Tim already knew how to milk because he helped milk Grandpa's cow in Archie. When they finished milking the fifteen cows, they'd filled about half of a 10-gallon can.

"Not bad for the first evening," commented Mr. Smith. They'll probably do even better tomorrow morning as they get use to us."

They turned the cows out to pasture and took the milk to the cream separator on the back porch. Betty, finished with her chores in the kitchen, volunteered to turn the handle. She had churned butter for her grandmother Smith and she liked to turn handles on things to see what miracles the machines produced. Mr. Smith set a 10-gallon milk can under the left spout of the separator and a 5-gallon cream can under the right spout. He poured the milk into the container on top of the separator, and as Betty turned the crank, beautiful yellow cream flowed into the cream can. A larger white stream of milk came out the other spout. When the cans filled, Tim and his father carried them to the cellar and put them into a brick enclosure containing blocks of ice. They left the milk buckets to soak, and washed up for supper.

As the aroma of fried ham stirred their appetites, Mrs. Smith led the family in a short prayer.

"Thank you Lord for giving us a safe trip through the storm today. We are thankful to be alive and healthy. Thank you for the Monroe family and bless them on their move to Harrisonville. Bless this food and help us as we start what may be the greatest adventure of our lives. In Jesus' name, Amen."

Everyone was so hungry they scarcely left any scraps for the dogs.

After supper, Mr. Smith lit the Aladdin lamp so Betty and Tim could see to wash the dishes, then lit a kerosene lantern to take out on the back porch so he and Mrs. Smith could see to clean the milk buckets and the cream separator. They quickly realized that cleaning and feeding chores would occupy much of their time on the farm. No one argued about heading to bed just as soon as they'd finished cleaning. It'd been a long day.

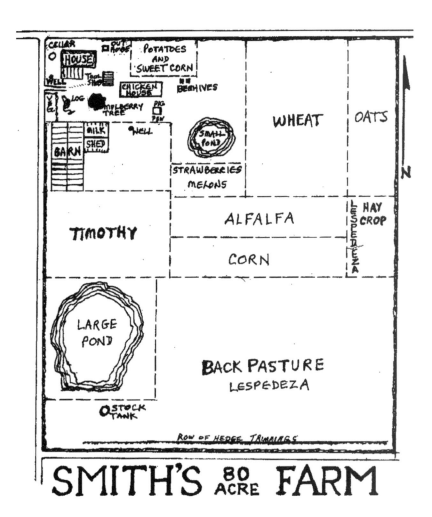

SMITH'S 80 ACRE FARM

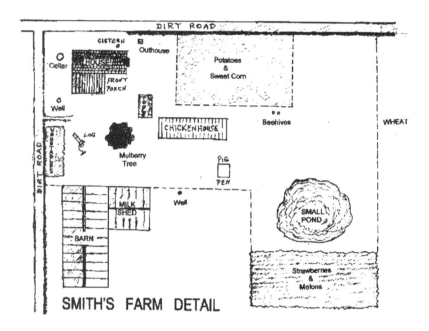

Farm House

Cass County
1931-1944

Garden Spot

Chapter 2—Getting Acquainted

On Thursday morning the Smith family heard rapid hoof beats. A teen-age boy rode up to their house on a beautiful brown and white stallion. Tim was on the front porch checking his fishing equipment.

"Hi there," the teenager said as he jumped off the stallion. I heard you were moving in and I wanted to be the first to welcome you to the Kingdom of Amarugia."

"We're glad to be here," Tim said as he extended his hand. "I'm Tim Smith and this is my sister, Betty. I'm twelve and Betty is thirteen. And what might your name be?"

"I'm Otto Swartz and I live about three quarters of a mile that way." He pointed to the north of the farm. "I just turned fifteen and let me tell you there are lots of things to see and do around here. Since I want to be King of Amarugia someday, I need to know all there is to know about this place, so if you like, I'll practice by telling you all about our Kingdom."

"Sounds good to me," replied Tim. "Is the fishing any good around here?"

"The fishing is great if you know where to go. I'll be glad to show you the best fishing holes and the best places to hunt, too. My dad owns the Fur Trading Post, so I have learned how to trap, too. There're deer, beaver, rabbits, squirrels, skunks, opossums, coons, prairie chickens, grouse, wild turkey, wolves, foxes, weasels, muskrats, snakes, and a lot of other animals in these hills and prairies. Some say there're even cougars and mountain lions in the Highlands." Betty's eyes widened as she wondered if he'd ever take a breath. "Over there, just to the west, is Owens Creek and the soil is good around here, too."

"So the soil's good, huh? That reminds me of a joke I heard about a dandelion. Do you know what happens when you give a dandelion an inch?"

"No, what happens?"

"It takes over a yard."

Otto smiled. "That's pretty good. I'll have to remember that one. We sure have lots of them in our yard."

"Do you have any brothers or sisters?" Betty asked.

"I have a little sister named Dovie, who's nine. Everybody loves Dovie, so I'm sure that even though you're older, you'll like her too."

"Great," said Betty. "I can't wait to meet her."

"What else is there to do around here?" asked Tim. "Are you in any group like the Boy Scouts?"

"Don't know anything about the Scouts, but I'm in 4-H."

"Does it cost anything to join?"

"It doesn't cost a penny but you have to bring your own animal if you're doing a livestock project. We keep records on our 4-H projects, so we'll learn how to do a super job and how to make a little moola on the side. We have contests and shows, which makes it fun and exciting, too. It's not all work. Sometimes we have games, refreshments, and music at our meetings. We meet lots of other kids just like us. Do you think you might like to join?"

Betty asked, "Can girls join the 4-H Club too?"

"Yes, they sure can; it's for both boys and girls." Betty paused to think on that one for a while, but then she smiled as she noticed a twinkle in Otto's eyes. She thought to herself, *"I'm going to like this guy a lot."*

Tim then asked, "When is the next 4-H meeting?"

Otto said, "Next Saturday over at the Browns' house. They have a son named Curley and a daughter named Martha. They're about our age."

Tim thought about what project he might take, and he asked Otto, "What's a project anyhow? It's not a class like we take in school, is it?"

"No, it's not like another school class and there are no tests. Take me for example—I'm taking one on horses and I help lead a project on fur trapping. It's doing things we like to do while we learn how to do them better and have a lot of fun at the same time."

Tim said, "I think I would like to take a calf for my project. I heard Dad say the other day that we needed to fatten a calf so we can have some beef to eat this winter. Our cows are a mixed breed of dairy and beef. I could take care of two calves; I could sell one and butcher the other."

Betty said, "I don't know if I'd rather do one on cooking or one on horses."

"Why not do both," suggested Otto. "Ask your folks and see what they say."

"Oh, by the way," Otto added, "Mom and Dad want to get acquainted with you all, and they asked me to invite your family to our house for dinner this Sunday. My mom will call your mom about it but they wanted you all to be thinking about it."

When Mr. and Mrs. Smith heard about Tim and Betty's interest in the 4-H Club, they were almost as excited as the kids.

"It's a great idea," their father enthused. "We can never learn too much about how to improve our farming skills and by sharing with others, we can help them and, in turn, they'll have suggestions which will help us, too."

Mrs. Smith said, "Honey, what do you know about this Pioneer Club?"

"From what I hear it's kind of like 4-H. Husbands and wives meet together with other couples and discuss better methods of farming and gardening. The club meets all year but more often in the fall and winter months when there is more time to meet. I'm all for joining!"

Tim and Betty went with Otto and Dovie to a 4-H meeting at the Browns' home and they really liked Curley and Martha Brown. They met several other kids their ages, including a girl with red hair named Sally, who also lived not far from the Smiths. They met several other kids who all went to the Oak Grove School. There were just too many names to remember at the first meeting, but they knew they would see them at school every day.

Before calling the meeting to order with the 4-H Pledge, the Browns let the kids play tree tag and softball. Once the meeting

15

got underway though, the youngsters shared their plans and details of their projects and then broke up into specific project groups. Betty and Sally, the red head, went to the one on cooking, and Otto and Tim went to the one on horses. As they rode in the buggy on the way back home, they could scarcely wait to tell their folks all about the meeting.

Later that week, Mr. Smith showed Tim which two calves he could fatten for his project. Betty asked her dad if he would have one of the mares bred to Lightning so she could have the offspring as a 4-H project. He agreed.

"Blaze is about ready to breed. You know it takes about 11 months before the offspring will be born."

"That's fine," Betty said. "Blaze can be my project and her baby will be next year's project."

"I like the way you think ahead, Betty-Boo!"

Betty smiled, pleased at the compliment. "May I also join the cooking club?" She knew this would please her mom and agreed with her when she once said, "When I cook a delicious dish of some kind, I feel just like an artist must feel when she paints a beautiful picture or how a musician feels when he plays or sings a beautiful song."

Mr. and Mrs. Smith were also pleased that Betty wanted to have Blaze and her upcoming foal as her main 4-H Club project for the year. She would keep records on all aspects of the gestation period along with reports of the care she gave her, food that she ate, and visits by the veterinarian.

Satisfied with her choices, Betty couldn't wait for the next meeting. The next evening, Mr. and Mrs. Smith had Betty and Tim heading to bed almost as soon as they finished the dishes after supper.

"You'll need to get up early to do your chores before your mother takes you to enroll in school," Mr. Smith reminded them gently.

Though they'd both met a few of their classmates at the Browns the previous meeting, Tim and Betty couldn't help but be a bit nervous when their roosters began crowing at sunrise. As

courtesy of Donald Lewis Osborn (1933-); photograph by Elsie Lydia Flanary (1903-1949), July 11, 1928
Oak Grove School in 1928
Windows on only one wall let daylight shine over students' left shoulders so no shadows interfered when writing with right hands. Steps for mounting a horse are at the extreme right in the picture.
The Oak Grove School House
was located near the center of Amarugia.

the boys milked the cows, Betty fed the chickens. She wanted to be sure she had plenty of time to be certain she looked just right. The smell of hot biscuits and gravy though, pulled them all to the kitchen like a magnet. While Betty helped clean up the breakfast dishes, Mrs. Smith encouraged Tim to brush his teeth with a little baking soda and flatten his hair with a bit of water.

Finally, by half past seven, the siblings and Mrs. Smith set off for the Oak Grove School with their records from Archie safely tucked away in Betty's satchel. Mrs. Smith had already made arrangements with Mrs. Swartz that they would pick up Dovie on the way to school this particular morning since the Swartz home lay halfway between the Smith home and the school. On the other school days, Otto would walk with them before he went to work at his father's store. They arrived at the Swartzs where Dovie had been waiting impatiently by the side of the road in front of their house.

"I'm so excited we'll be able to go to school together, Betty! Oh, I love that ribbon in your hair. Miss Rogers is really nice, you'll see! I bet you're smart. She'll let you help dust the erasers and maybe help teach the little ones! Tim, maybe you'll get to sit with Curley! Hey, What happened to your hair? I think...."

"C'mon, hop in, Dovie. I'm sure Miss Rogers doesn't like her students to be tardy!"

When they arrived, they tied Blaze to a tree and entered the door of the one-room school. Miss Rogers greeted them all warmly and Betty gave her the papers she had in her satchel. Miss Rogers said she appreciated getting this information and looked forward to being their teacher. She showed Betty and Tim their desks where they could put their supplies. She told Mrs. Smith she would be sending a note home with information about the school. Other pupils began to arrive, so Mrs. Smith left for home. She was impressed with the way Miss Rogers greeted each of them with a knowing question about their weekend activities. Before long, the Smith children knew the names of all 25 students.

One day, Otto took Tim, Betty, and Dovie to school in the Swartzs' big buggy. As they rode along, the girls chattering in the seat behind them, Otto turned to Tim, "How about me telling you some things about Amarugia so you'll know this place better?"

"Sure—anything's better than that racket back there!"

Otto laughed, "How's this for history? Supposedly the famous Spanish explorer, Ponce-de-Leon, may have spent the winter in the Amarugia Highlands way back in 1513, and some say he and his men explored these hills at that time just like we are planning to do."

"Do you think he buried any treasure here to hide it from the Indians?"

"He might have. Who knows? But I haven't stumbled across any yet."

"How do you pronounce this place where you live?"

"It is usually pronounced Am-a-ROO-GEE as if it were spelled A-m-a-r-o-o-g-e-e," Otto replied.

"This isn't the only place with that name is it?"

"There's a place in northwest Missouri spelled A-m-a-r-u-g-a-h, which was a ghost town and up near Gentry. It's also been known as Jackson's Mill, Mervin's Mill, and Waddeville. Some say the Indians there at the time may have named it Amarugah, which means 'site of friends'; others say it means 'an unsavory place'."

"Which tribe of Indians?" asked Tim.

"Folks think the Osage Indian tribe was one of the first to live in Cass County. The Kansa, Delaware, and Shawnee have also been in this area. We find arrowheads all the time. Then around 1830, a man by the name of Basy Owens explored this area. He was an agent of the Hudson Bay Fur Company and started a fur trading post here. Families from eastern Kentucky, eastern Tennessee, and western Virginia moved into these hills. Others started coming from places like Indiana, Ohio, and Illinois. They liked the flat lands next to Amarugia which we call the Prairie. It wasn't long before they realized some form of government was needed to settle arguments, so they got a council together and this guy, Basy Owens, was declared King. Why they decided upon a monarchy, I don't know, and I have not been able to find anyone who does know. They must have felt a need for some law and order so they decided to do it this way."

"Well, for a time it worked out fine, but they soon discovered that there were fewer furbearing animals than they had thought, and some of the trappers also lived on the prairie. Stories are told about invasions into Amarugia by some groups from Indiana, Illinois, and Ohio who had moved into the prairie which was to the south and southeast of the Amarugia Highlands area. This nearly destroyed the colony. One time the King was captured and held prisoner for several years, hoping to get a heavy ransom for his release. But he got sick and died. Owens II, his descendent, became King. At first there was a lot of stealing livestock back and forth, so the King fined the thieves—usually just a pumpkin or a chicken or a jug of cider. It seemed to work pretty well. I guess it was pretty peaceful for awhile."

"Awhile? What happened? It hasn't been peaceful ever since?" asked Tim.

"Afraid not," answered Otto. "After the death of Owens II, the only descendent they could crown 'King' was old and blind. No way could he be King. The Council met and elected a guy by the name of Sir Thomas Bundy. At this time the people decided that a King should wear a King's crown. He was a stern ruler, yet just but fair in all his official acts. He finally moved away and appointed Jacob Weddington to fill his place. Now Weddington was bald-headed and the people said that he could not serve as King unless he would submit to having the crown glued to his head when he was presiding in court. When Weddington refused, David Wilson declared himself King and is still ruling the Kingdom of Amarugia."

"Wow! That's really somethin'," said Tim. "I have lived less than 10 miles from here and this is the first time I've heard about any of this."

"I'm not surprised," Otto said. "There was so much killing and mistrust during the Civil War time, folks around here didn't know whom they could trust, so even today they keep to themselves. As a matter of fact there are very few people who will admit they even live in Amarugia. You may ask why and I guess it's because they assume other people think they are always fussing and fighting or are backward acting or something. I've studied Amarugia's history so I can be the best King possible. I figure if I know all about how to be a King and let people know I'd like to do this, then I can take King David Wilson's place when he moves on or dies."

By this time they'd almost reached the school house.

"Thanks for giving me such a great run-down on this area of Cass County! Well, guess this is it. See you after school."

"You sure are a good listener, Tim. Thanks for letting me practice on you. Yep, I'll see you after school today—though usually I have to stay at the Trading Post till my dad closes it. Good luck today!"

"OK. See ya!"

"Bye, Dovie! Betty, have a good day!"

"You too, Otto," the girls called as they hurried off toward the ringing bell.

Chapter 3—Rattlesnake Hill

Otto rode up Tim's driveway right after breakfast. He let his pony, Lightning, gallop at full speed as he gave a secret whistle he and Tim had agreed upon so they could recognize each other even before one was in sight of the other. Tim appeared and they made plans for the day.

As usual, Tim had a joke ready. "Have you heard the one about the wife who said to her husband, 'I baked two kinds of cookies today. Would you like to take your pick?'"

"No, what did he say?"

"He said, 'No thanks. I'll use my hammer.'"

"That's funny," said Otto, "But don't tell that one to our mothers; they might stop baking us cookies."

"Don't worry about that. I haven't had a bad cookie in my life."

Otto said, "How 'bout we check out a hill not far from my house that looks like an Indian mound?"

"Sounds great, as long as I get back before dark to help with the chores."

As they rode along, Tim wondered aloud, "What was it like around here when this part was first discovered?"

"Some say the Spaniards hid some money in the Amarugia Highlands, and I've also heard that Confederate money has been found here, too."

Tim's eyes got big as he said, "I've never even seen Confederate money, or much money of any kind, really."

"Maybe we'll stumble on some today," Otto added.

They continued on a dirt road beside a row of hedge bushes—a common type of fence used on many of the farms in Amarugia. Inexpensive, it could be maintained by trimming with a hedge knife and patched with some of the thorny branches. The leftover branches

21

were tossed into brush piles which made great hiding places for rabbits while the larger trees sheltered squirrels and turtledoves.

Otto asked, "Would you like to know what happened here during the Civil War?"

"Sure."

"Missouri—like everyone—suffered a lot in the Civil War. About 100,000 men enlisted in the Federal army and more than 50,000 joined the Rebels. Even though Missouri didn't secede from the Union, Missouri has a star on the Confederate flag anyway."

"No kidding. I didn't know that!" said Tim, surprised.

"We had more battles in Missouri than all the other states except for Virginia and Tennessee. There were also lots of fights in Kansas, just across the border. It was called the Missouri-Kansas Border War."

"What's Kansas got to do with Amarugia?"

"I'm getting there. Have you ever heard of a guy named William Quantrill?"

"Was he one of the Kings?"

"No, he was the leader of a Confederate guerrilla band. Neighbors killed his father for no good reason, it seems. Also the fathers of the James brothers and Cole Younger were killed. On August 21, 1863, Quantrill and his men burned most of the town of Lawrence, Kansas, killing something like 150 men. It's said that on that day Jesse James' brother, Frank, rode with them. The Federal government believed Quantrill's Raiders and other Southern sympathizers headed this way to hide out in Cass County and get help from some of the locals. So General Thomas Ewing,—the brother-in-law of General Sherman who made that famous march across Georgia,—issued Order Number 11 on August 25, 1863."

"I've heard a little bit about that," said Tim, "They say it was called 'Total War' when everything in the area was destroyed."

"That's exactly what happened here. Order Number 11 forced all civilians in Jackson, Cass, Bates, and northern Vernon County to leave. Everyone here in Cass County living more than a mile from Harrisonville or Pleasant Hill had to leave their homes within 15 days. The people of Amarugia went to Harrisonville, about 10 miles northeast of here. More than 20,000 people had to leave. Union troops took all the food and burned everything to the ground. Only the chimneys were left standing. The chimneys which remained were called 'Jennison's Tombstones' after the Kansas Jayhawk leader 'Doc' Jennison whose troops did much of the burning and looting. One of the few places that survived in what came to be called the 'Burnt District' was the 1835 Sharp-Hopper Log Cabin. It was built over 30 years before the war."

"Wow, how do you remember all this stuff? I wish I knew all you know about Amarugia."

"Well, when Dad moved here from Kentucky, he got hold of lots of old newspapers from some of the locals and studied them, and now I study them all the time to learn all I can about Amarugia. I reread the newspaper articles and then I practice on guys like you."

By this time, Tim was getting hungry. Hearing his stomach growl, Otto laughed. "I'm hungry, too. C'mon, I know where there are some really good blackberries."

The boys urged the pony and mule into lively trots, and they soon arrived at a large patch of blackberries in a ditch along the side of the road. The boys found a large shade tree nearby where they put halters on their mounts and let them graze. After they picked a couple of handfuls of blackberries, they took them to a shady spot where they munched on them, along with some cookies. Otto glanced out of the corner of his eye and said, "Oh, no! Here comes somebody!"

Tim looked up and saw a heavyset lady with what looked like a long switch in her hand. Walking at a lively pace, she swished the switch with every step as she made her way toward them.

"Do you know her?" Tim asked.

"No, I don't know her, but I think we had better get out of here in a hurry or we are going to get acquainted. She must think all the blackberries in the ditch belong to her."

The boys shoved the rest of the blackberries into their mouths, put the bridles on their mounts, and raced in the opposite direction as fast as Lightening and Thunder could gallop.

"Let's go look at that Indian mound you told me about," Tim said.

"Sure, it's not far from here as the crow flies."

"Have you been there before?"

"No, I don't go much anywhere by myself. My parents say traveling alone can be dangerous. They're worried about leftover bushwhackers from the war, and Indians in these hills looking for deer and things."

"What's your definition of a bushwhacker anyway?"

"A person who attacks by ambush, a guerrilla fighter."

Otto enjoyed answering Tim's questions. He also had other reasons for going on these rides. He not only enjoyed Tim's friendship, but he also thought Tim's sister, Betty, was very pretty. Otto hoped to ask Betty for a date when the time was right, if he could muster up enough courage. No one likes to be rejected, and he wanted to wait until he was reasonably sure she would go out with him before he asked her. After all, a future King should expect people to say "Yes" to his requests.

Soon they came to the base of what looked like a tall Indian mound. As soon as they dismounted and tied Lightning and Thunder to a couple of trees, Tim challenged, "I'll race you to the top," as he took off running as fast as he could go, but Otto had longer legs and reached the top first.

"I'm here," Otto called out.

Tim arrived at the top of the hill huffing and puffing. "It feels good to run. I was getting tired of riding all the time."

"Tim, look out behind you!" Otto shouted. "There's a big rattlesnake on that rock next to you!"

Tim whirled around and sure enough there was a big fat rattlesnake sunning himself on a flat rock.

"Oh man!" Tim yelled! "And look to your left! There's another one over there!" Just about everywhere they looked they saw snakes stretched out on the rocks enjoying themselves in the warm sunlight.

"Let's get out of here!" both boys yelled in unison.

They took off running for the bottom of the hill. Once at the bottom, Otto said, "We can look for treasure some day when it is cold and those snakes won't be taking a sun bath!"

Tim said as he panted, "That makes us even now. You won the race to the top of the hill, but I beat you back down."

Otto smiled. He really never felt he was in competition with Tim, but he appreciated having a friend with a good sense of humor, as well as someone with ambition to do his best at whatever he attempted.

On the way back to Tim's house, Otto said, "In addition to rattlesnakes, we also have copperhead snakes, and cottonmouth water moccasins, and they're all poisonous. The doctor in Everett has treated a lot of people for snake bites."

"I sure hope we never need to see him for that!"

"Me, too. Hey, have you heard about Old Dot?"

"No. Who's she?"

"People say she talks with the dead. People go visit her for answers from the dead. Sometimes she has no answers." Tim looked skeptical.

"My dad took me with him to one of these meetings one night. It turned out to be one of those times when she said she couldn't get any answers. I heard she had a short cane she hid under her apron and she tapped the answers with it. I think she was trying to make money off of people who were curious and superstitious."

"So nothing happened?"

"Not a thing; then there's Granddad Horton."

"Granddad Horton?"

"He moved here from Kentucky a while back. Supposedly he had a mystical power that could stop bleeding."

Once more Tim looked at Otto, doubt all over his face.

"One day Edie Garrett cut her arm bad. Blood was spurting everywhere! She's out there screaming her head off and Granddad Horton, calm as you please, just held her hand and muttered a few words. The bleeding stopped and she healed right up. Not even a scar."

"So why isn't he the doctor 'round here?"

"I think most folks were kind of afraid of him the way my mom tells it. He could have taught this power to another person but only to a girl and I guess his daughter-in-law just couldn't get it through her head. Neighbors sometimes called him in as a doctor but he died without passing on his secret."

When they returned from their ride and Tim headed home, Tim thought,

"This has got to be the most interesting place I've ever been. I'm glad I have a good friend like Otto to tell me about Amarugia."

Chapter 4—Quilting Bee

While the boys were making their getaway from Rattlesnake Hill, the girls had settled into the easy folds of what had become their quilting bee. Some of the neighbors had brought feed sacks and even their own designs when they joined the meeting.

Betty wanted to make a quilt with designs of all the animals they had on the farm. Sally liked to draw, and offered to draw the animal patterns, and soon the other girls added their suggestions to her list. Dovie wanted to make a small quilt for her bed with drawings of the fur bearing animals her dad and Otto handled at the Fur Trading Post. Though only nine, she had a very independent streak and insisted on making her patterns. Some of her animal designs were unusual looking but she knew what they were, and that's what counted the most. One of the older ladies showed the younger girls how to appliqué, by sewing a cutout piece of cloth onto another piece. Once they tucked the edges under, they sewed the design onto the larger piece of cloth either with small, hidden stitches or ornamental stitches.

While they also used what they made to cover chairs and benches, they spent most of their time on linens. When they worked on a bed quilt, they stretched three layers of material over the round or rectangular quilting frame to keep the fabrics smooth and in shape. Following the design marked on the top layer, they used small stitches so that the interlining would not slip, before binding the edges with strips of cloth to make the seams.

While they sewed, Mrs. Swartz shared the story of how she met her husband at the Fur Trading Post one winter's day some sixteen years ago. "Word got to our village that a man had started up a fur trading place where we could sell our pelts. After my mother died from a bad fever, as the only child, I was the only one left to care for my father when he took ill. I noticed that Mr. Swartz, Karl, always treated me like any other trader and was more than fair when he purchased our pelts."

"You fell in love just by doing business with him?" Betty asked.

"Oh no, dear. That came later! I told him I was learning English and wondered if he had any old *Cass County Democrat* newspapers I could borrow to help my studies. Turns out he'd been collecting them in order to learn more about the area and he offered to share them with me. It wasn't long before he started coming over to our village and we studied together. He was patient and kind and funny, and when I realized all that, I realized I'd fallen in love with him."

A chorus of gleeful sighs rose from the girls. "Tell the rest, Mama," Dovie urged.

"Well, obviously I wasn't the only one who fell in love. One evening I came in to prepare supper for my father and found him already eating—with Karl! I suppose he wasn't so sure my father would give his permission, so he brought all sorts of goodies from the Trading Post. The whole tribe had told my father what a fair man Karl had proved to be to our tribe, so of course he didn't object! We married two weeks later, and I'm so grateful my father lived to see it. Within a few more weeks he passed. A new chief was selected, but I do not know him or his family."

"What a lovely story," Mrs. Johnson practically cooed. "Do the children see their Indian relatives?"

"By the time we had children, it had been months since we'd been to the village, so no, they've never met them. Most of my Indian relatives moved on to Oklahoma."

Still giggly from Dovie's mother's love story, talk quickly turned among the girls to the upcoming box supper. This was a big fundraiser for school supplies that always caused a stir and plenty of boy-talk. "I sure hope Tim buys my box." Sally shyly admitted. Betty quickly responded.

"How will he know which box is yours?"

"Oh, that will be easy. I'll have a picture of a beautiful Jersey cow on it."

Everybody smiled because they knew nobody else could draw a Jersey cow like Sally, and Tim would have to be blind not to spot it. Betty secretly hoped Otto would buy her box. She had decided to prepare fried capon chicken breasts when she overheard Otto say it was his favorite meat. She also planned to make some deviled eggs and her grandmother's potato salad. For dessert she'd pack some of her mother's fudge. The organizers would provide the apple cider and tea to drink.

"Sally, I'll make sure Tim knows about your box."

"Really, Betty?" she squealed. "I'd be ever so grateful!"

After the others had left the quilting bee, Betty confided in her mom.

"I'll just die if Otto doesn't buy my box. What if he buys some other girl's box or what if he doesn't buy a box at all?"

"Betty, life is too short to worry about all the 'what-ifs.' Just prepare the best and prettiest box you know how and eat with whoever buys it. Everything will work out O.K. It usually does."

Chapter 5 — Bull Attack

"How would you boys like to earn some money trimming hedge?" Mr. Smith asked Otto and Tim.

"Sure, Dad."

"I don't know about you, Tim, but I sure could use some extra money for that box supper coming up this weekend. When do we start?"

"Some of the calves have been getting out in our back pasture by slipping through holes in the hedge fence. You boys could trim the hedge branches and plug up the holes in a couple of days. Does one dollar a day sound fair?"

"Yes sir! It's a deal," they chimed in unison.

"Tim, you know where the trimming knives are. Get to it, then. I'll see you boys up at the house for dinner at noon."

The boys stopped by the barn to grab the knives—each about two and one-half feet long with a blade about four inches wide.

"Can I leave Lightning in the pasture?"

"Sure, no problem."

"You know we've got an Angus bull out there, but if we don't stir him up, he usually behaves."

The dogs, Jack and Pumpkin, trailed behind them as they headed to the back pasture.

"When we go in for dinner I'll get my rifle so we can bring back some squirrels and rabbits when we finish working. Our moms can use them to make mulligan stew."

"Let's plug up the holes in the hedge row first. Then we'll toss the rest of the trimmings onto the row of dead branches already there on the ground from the last trimming. OK?" suggested Otto.

"Sounds good to me." Tim agreed, "Hey, have you heard the joke about the boy who met his neighbor at the country store?"

"I don't think so."

"The neighbor lady said, 'I am looking forward to seeing your mother at the Pioneer Club meeting tomorrow and thanking her for that delicious pie you brought me yesterday.'"

"Yes ma'am," the boy said, "But would you mind thanking her for *two* pies?"

Otto laughed and they started to work. In a couple of hours they had plugged up all the holes they could find.

While the boys worked, Jack and Pumpkin checked out the row of dead branches where rabbits made their nests. Pumpkin, small enough to go into the row, scared out a rabbit and Jack ran him down. They carried it over to a shade tree and had their breakfast.

"Just before we quit work this evening, I'll put Pumpkin into some of the piles of old hedge branches so she can run out some more rabbits. We can shoot a couple of them apiece to take to our moms. Dad said we can probably find some squirrels on the other side of the pasture where the tall hedge and nut trees are. Grandpa Smith has told us where most of the squirrels hang out."

"That sounds like fun," said Otto, "and then we can take a quick dip in the pond."

"You bet," said Tim, "I never forget to do that!"

At noon they went in and ate a nice chicken dinner with Tim's folks and Betty, then returned to the pasture for more hedge trimming. Eventually, Tim looked over to Otto. "What time do you think it is?" Otto stuck his hedge knife in the ground and looked at the shadow it made.

"It looks about 3:30 or 4:00 o'clock to me," he said.

"We're about half done with the hedge, so I bet we can finish it up tomorrow. Let's stick Pumpkin in the brush pile and have her run us out some rabbits. I'll put a leash on Jack and tie him to a hedge bush so we won't shoot him by accident. Do you want to go first?"

"Sure."

Tim steered Pumpkin into the maze of tunnels in the old hedge pile. Almost immediately out ran a rabbit. Otto cocked the rifle; took careful aim and brought the rabbit down with the first shot. "Pretty good. Couldn't have done better myself," Tim said. Otto shot another one and then said, "It's your turn now. Come here Pumpkin. You're a good girl. Let me put you in this section. It looks like there should be some rabbits in there." Tim got his rifle ready and sure enough a rabbit ran out and Tim fired away. Jack barked and tugged at his leash but Tim's bullet hit the ground an inch or so behind the rabbit.

"Try again." Otto encouraged him; "Go ahead. Reload and I'll put Pumpkin in a little farther down the way. The next time when a rabbit comes out, aim about an inch in front of his nose."

Tim hit it easily. He then shot one more. Tim said, "We've got four rabbits—that's two apiece. Let's walk across the pasture and see if we can get four squirrels. That should give our moms enough for stew."

"I think that'll be plenty."

"Good. Now keep your eye out for our bull, Captain Midnight. If he starts snorting and pawing the ground, it means it's time for us to get out of here. We can sic Jack and Pumpkin on him, but Dad doesn't like for us to do that unless it's absolutely necessary."

On the other side of the pasture where the taller hedge and nut trees were growing, they found plenty of squirrel nests tucked in the hickory and oak trees. Four dead squirrels later they raced toward the pond.

When Mr. Smith met them as they returned from their swim, he was pleased to hear about the progress they'd made on the fence.

"Tomorrow, I'd like for you boys to yoke the two calves that have been getting out on the road through some holes in the hedge fence. You've proven yourselves on the mending and trimming so I'm sure you'll do just as good a job with this."

Leading them back to the barn, he showed them two yokes he had made from strong hedge sticks. Each of them was in the shape of a "Y" which they could attach around the calf's neck.

"Take plenty of heavy cord so the yoke will stay on and not hurt the calf's neck," he added.

"I'll bring my lasso," Otto said, "I need the practice." He picked up his half of the rabbits and squirrels and headed home for the evening.

After dressing the rabbits and squirrels and helping with the evening milking chores, Tim joined his family for supper. Betty reminded him that the school Pie and Box Supper was coming up this Saturday evening. Even though Otto had mentioned it that morning, Tim had already forgotten about it – he just wasn't very interested in girls yet. He was still trying to figure them out! But he was good friends with Sally, and Betty told him Sally was going to make some divinity for her box. When he found out divinity wasn't something religious but a white candy, he decided to buy her box.

"Now don't forget to remind Otto of the box supper coming up tomorrow evening," Betty said, hoping she sounded casual. "It raises lots of money for the school, you know."

Otto arrived at eight o'clock the next morning, lasso in hand. With the dogs leading the way, they took their hedge knives and the two wooden yokes and walked to the back pasture. They had no problem spotting the renegade calves already sticking their heads into the newly-patched hedge fence trying to bore a hole in it.

"Looks like they're trying to break out of the pasture for a new adventure," Otto observed.

"They're going to have a new adventure all right," Tim said as he laid the yokes down and Otto began to twirl the lasso. Tim had Jack and Pumpkin stay between them and the cattle, especially Captain Midnight. If the cattle started toward them, Tim planned to sic Jack and Pumpkin on them.

The calves were just the right size – not so small that the yoke would hamper their walking, yet small enough for the boys to wrestle to the ground. Otto tossed the noose of his lasso over the head of the first calf and threw him to the ground. The calf made a little noise but not enough to excite the cows and bull on the other side of the pasture. As soon as they tied the calf's feet so he couldn't get away, they put on the yoke, tied it with heavy cord, and turned the calf loose.

"I've never lassoed a calf before." Tim offered. "I tried to lasso Jack once, but he didn't like it and I only got the one chance. Can I try anyway?"

"Sure," Otto said, "But let's go ahead and cut a little hedge first and give the other calf time to settle down. I'll show you how to hold and sling the lasso."

"Aw. C'mon. The hedge can wait. You can show me now!"

"I think it's better that we work on the hedge for now. You know the saying, 'All good things come to him who waits.'"

"Yeah, you sound like my grandpa, who also says, 'None of us ever gets patience. We just need to learn how to practice it.' I guess you're right."

They worked a good five or six feet of hedge until Otto finally suggested they take a break, and demonstrated how to use the lasso. Satisfied with Tim's progress, Otto felt his friend was ready to try. "I'll move over between him and the other cattle so he won't run away from you."

Imitating Otto, Tim made a slow warm up motion, twirled the lariat and tossed it at the calf's head. The rope hit the calf's shoulder and slid off. The calf looked smug, like he'd fooled everyone. Tim quickly tossed the lasso two more times and on the third try, finally got him. The calf backed up until the rope began to choke him. Then he started bawling. It didn't take long for his cries to reach the herd. Captain Midnight answered by bellowing, snorting, and pawing the ground. The cows stopped grazing, lifted their heads, and came together in a group. As the calf continued crying out, the bull snorted, pawed the ground some more, and started running toward the boys and the calf. The boys held the calf on the ground but he continued to bawl as they finished attaching the yoke. Still bellowing, the bull broke into a gallop and tore across the pasture toward them. Mr. Smith, hearing the commotion from the adjoining field where he was working, realized the bull was charging. He quickly tied the team of mules to the fence at the end of the row and vaulted over the wire separating him from the back pasture. Running toward the boys, he shouted, "Grab the bull's ring and twist it! Whatever you do, don't let go!"

As the bull bore down on them, Tim called out, "Sic him Jack! Sic him Pumpkin!" The dogs immediately ran toward the bull. Pumpkin nipped at his head and Jack at his heels. Trying to shake them off, Captain Midnight lowered his head and caught Pumpkin on her side and tossed her almost three feet in the air. She yelped but got up and limped her way back to the fray where she continued harassing the bull. Otto tossed his lasso over Captain Midnight's head and, falling to one knee, he pulled with all his might. Captain Midnight's head lowered and his neck twisted as he went down on his front knees. Tim quickly grabbed the bullring and twisted hard until the bull's nose started bleeding. In pain, the bull rolled on his side and continued to bellow. Mr. Smith ran up and carefully tied the end of the lasso to the bullring.

"Great job boys! Let's let him simmer down a little. He was just doing what he thought was his duty to protect the calves. You know, we haven't had cattle stolen like some people. I think when people see that ring in the bull's nose they know we have a mean bull. Now let's see about those calves. You boys did a good job yoking them."

"I lassoed the second one all by myself," bragged Tim.

"Let's go in a little early this evening. The box supper's tonight and the cows won't give as much milk anyway after all this excitement. I'll lead Captain Midnight back over to the other side of the pasture so he can be with the cows."

"Thanks, Dad."

"Thanks, Mr. Smith."

"No, thank you, boys. You did me proud back there."

Still beaming from his father's compliment, Tim turned to Otto, "Betty wanted me to be sure and ask if you were going to the box supper."

"I wouldn't miss it for anything. Is Betty taking a box?"

"She sure is. She's been working on it all week!"

"Have you seen it? I want to be sure I bid on the right one!"

"*What was Otto going on about,*" thought Tim, "*It's just a box with some chicken in it for heaven's sake!*" Out loud he said to his friend, "She's had that box done for weeks. It's blue and has pictures of red flowers on it. There is a blue curvy trim along the edge. Does that help?"

"It sure does. Thanks, buddy. See ya this evening."

"Yeah. See ya tonight," answered Tim, still wondering what the big deal was.

Chapter 6 — Box Supper

The week of the box supper, Tim had taken on Betty's chores of feeding the chickens and gathering the eggs so Betty could help her mother prepare the pies, cakes, and boxes for the big event. Mrs. Smith baked and iced two lovely angel food cakes, and baked half a dozen pies—apple, peach and blackberry.

Saturday evening, the Smith family piled into the buggy. A flurry of activity met them when they arrived at the school. Families caught up with their visiting in the schoolyard while hitching their horses, ponies, and mules to the nearby oak trees. From inside the school house came the sounds of piano music and people visiting. The cake walk had already begun when the Smiths entered the doorway, and the fragrance of cakes and pies pulled Tim in line to try to win a cake. He paid the fee to play five times. He began to realize that his money was going more quickly than he had planned, but when he won a cake he knew he wouldn't go hungry. He planned to bid on Sally's box and hoped he still had enough money to buy it. When the cake walk ended, the chairman of the school board made a few announcements and said words of praise for Miss Rogers who was returning for her second year of teaching at Oak Grove. She received a lot of applause for teaching all 25 kids in grades one through eight in the one-room schoolhouse. She did look sort of tired, but she looked happy. She said she appreciated everyone coming and all the hard work they'd done, and thanked them for raising so much money for the much needed supplies. Then, the auctioneer for the night took the stage and started auctioning off the boxes made by the younger girls—those in the fourth and fifth grades. Next came the boxes of girls in the sixth, seventh, and eighth grades. Betty whispered a reminder in Tim's ear about which was Sally's box. Finally, the auctioneer held up Sally's box. Tim quickly discovered that some of the older boys also wanted to eat with her. It didn't take long for Tim to realize he'd indeed spent too much money at the cake walk and couldn't outbid the other boys. He was too short to see who finally made the highest bid for her box. He felt like his fun for the evening was over if he couldn't eat with Sally and wanted to kick himself for spending so much money on the cakewalk.

Before long, Betty's box was being auctioned. Otto knew most of the boys there and when the auctioneer held up her box, three or four boys quickly bid on it. Otto was glad he'd made some extra money working for Mr. Smith. The boys knew that Otto liked Betty and they were determined to run up the price. When the price got up to $2.00, Otto stopped bidding for awhile. When it got to $2.20, he noticed one of the boys raised his hands in the air, shaking his head to let his friend on the other side of the room know that was all the money he had. The other boy indicated he couldn't bid any higher either.

Otto waited until he heard the auctioneer shout, "Going once; going twice and…." Just then Otto shouted, "I bid two and a quarter!" Then the auctioneer said, "Going once, going twice, and sold to that young gentleman for two twenty-five!" Otto smiled and relaxed for the first time that evening.

Then it came time to eat. Each girl sat at one of the desks with the person who purchased her box. Otto and Betty smiled and laughed as they realized they had achieved their goal of being together and helping with the school expenses all at the same time.

"Those guys had me scared." Otto admitted. "I thought I might have to sell Lightning to be able to buy your box!" They both had a big laugh. After they had each eaten the delicious capon meat off the wishbones, Otto suggested they break his first to see who would get a secret wish. "The one left holding the longest piece gets his wish," reminded Otto. As they positioned their fingers and thumbs, Otto quickly put pressure on his thumb and two fingers which caused the wishbone to break and he was left holding the longest piece.

"Let's do the other one too," he suggested. This time, he hesitated a second, which gave Betty time to put plenty of pressure on her thumb and fingers, and she ended up with the longest part of the wishbone.

"Now," he said, "We each have a wish to make. Let's make our secret wish and remember, if you don't tell anyone, it's supposed to come true."

They paused and silently made their wishes, and then smiled at each other with a twinkle in their eyes. Pointing at the door, Betty asked, "Who is that person coming in?" Otto turned to look, and Betty leaned over and planted a kiss on his cheek and whispered, "Thanks for buying my box!"

Otto blushed as he turned around. Then he kissed Betty squarely on her lips, holding it for two or three seconds, before replying, "And thanks for being such a sweetheart!" Now it was her turn to blush.

For a while after they had eaten, Otto introduced Betty to other people whom she had not yet met. Then Otto said, "You know I've been to your house a lot of times to see Tim, and we are friends that way but I would like to ask you something. Would you be my girlfriend? I really like you a lot and we're both interested in many of the same things."

"Yes, I'd love to be your girlfriend. I thought you'd never ask."

"That's great! And I promise not to take you anywhere where trouble is likely to break out. It seems like there is a fight here in Amarugia every Saturday night after the dance. A big fight took place at the Alec Lopeman's house around 1890. Do you want to hear about it?"

"Sure, what happened?"

"Two 'outsiders' (non-Amarugians) became unfriendly. A man known as Ab knifed Lee Nichols. Ab was known to have killed three or four men but always said it was self-defense. It's said that this time he used a 30-cent Barlow knife—they had good knives back then—and sliced diagonally down across Nichols' chest. He wasn't wearing a coat, but did have on some thick underwear, a stiff bosom shirt...."

"What's a bosom shirt?" Asked Betty, confused.

41

"It's like a board down the front—and a watch chain. Supposedly, Ab managed to cut the chain in two or three places and his insides rolled right out!"

"Eeeew! Otto!"

"Sorry. Guess that was kind of gory. Should I stop?"

"Well, now I want to know what happened!"

"O.K., so Ab sent a man for a doctor who sewed up the victim and he lived. I've heard that the knife clipped off the ends of two ribs which Nichols somehow managed to preserve in a jar of alcohol as souvenirs."

"My goodness! I'm perfectly happy not to go to dances and parties like that either. I like the Virginia Reel they do at 4-H and that is enough for me."

"Would you like for me to drive you home this evening?"

"That would be great. Let me ask my Mom and I'll get right back to you."

In a few minutes Betty returned and said, "We've got our first date! My wishbone wish has come true."

"Mine too," chimed in Otto as he smiled.

Tim was told by his parents that they had purchased Sally's box and he could have it in exchange for the cake he had won in the cake walk. He was more than glad to do this and he and Sally also had a great time at the Oak Grove Box Supper.

Jim Arnold looks at Owens Creek
which runs through his farm in Amarugia.

SUMMER — 1910

Chapter 7 — Much to Learn

As spring eased its way into summer, Dovie's mare named "Mummy" was becoming heavy with a new offspring. Betty's horse Blaze's belly continued to grow with her first foal as well. Both girls were so excited they could hardly stand it. They told everybody about it and the entire community seemed to catch their enthusiasm.

Otto galloped almost the whole way to Tim's house. He sprang from Lightning and tapped three times on the farmhouse door. Just as he'd hoped, Betty opened the door shining her wonderful smile. Otto felt his heart jump and at first he was at a loss for words.

"Hi, Otto, glad to see you. How's your summer?"

"I'm having a great summer. How's your summer coming along?"

"Great, I love living out here in the country."

Tim came in. "You're right on time. Thunder's hitched out back and ready to go. All I have to say is 'Roll, Thunder roll' and she will follow Lightning anywhere."

Otto turned to Tim's mom, "I'm going to show Tim some good places to fish along Owens Creek and some good ponds in the area. As my grandpa says, 'If a person wants to grow up and amount to anything, he needs to go fishing once in a while.'"

"Your grandpa sounds like a wise man," Mrs. Smith smiled. "Have fun, boys!"

Tim grabbed his lunch and they waved goodbye as they dashed off for another adventure.

"Hey, Otto, this morning, I heard something which sounded like a man yelling. Dad heard it too. It seemed to come from someplace north of here, kind of west of the school. Do you have any idea what it could be?"

"You probably heard someone who was being punished by King David's Court. They usually hold court at nine o'clock on Saturday mornings and sometimes during the week they have midnight court. King David made a Royal Proclamation, and since I plan to become king someday, I carry a copy with me."

Otto reached into the bib pocket of his overalls and pulled out an article from the *Cass County Democrat*. As they rode along, he told Tim about the article.

"It was written at his palace in the royal city of Everett. To sum it up, he first gives the names of the men who will enforce the King's rule. He calls these men High Muck-a-Mucks and gives them full authority to maintain order. He says that the people are being given a mild and gentle government which has been the envy of their neighbors. He goes on to say that he gives power to these High Muck-a-Mucks so they'll be a holy terror to evil doers. If anyone mistreats any of our good subjects, he's empowered and instructed these High Muck-a-Mucks to inflict upon each of the offenders, the Bastinado, morning, noon, and night, daily for a calendar month."

"Wow," Tim said, "What's the Bastinado?"

"A form of oriental torture that involves a beating with a stick or cane, usually on the soles of the feet. Can you imagine how sore your feet would be if they were beaten thirty times with sticks or canes three times a day for a month?"

"*I hope this never happens to* me!" thought Tim.

By this time they came to a ford crossing Owens creek, and Otto pointed out some places where bullhead and channel catfish lurked.

"A brush pile or a log in the creek usually marks a good place to fish, and if you want to catch really big ones, you need to come here when the creek gets low and reach under the boulders and pull them out by their gills. It's called 'hogging' and my dad said that one time he pulled out one that weighed almost twenty pounds."

"Twenty pounds? With his bare hands?" asked Tim doubting.

"Yessiree," Otto confirmed proudly. "He nailed the fish's tail to a tree and filleted it on the spot. Just a few yards to the right of here is a deep pool about twenty feet across where you can catch carp, sun perch, catfish and suckers."

Tim reached down and picked up an acorn from under one of the large oak trees.

"Do you know how a little acorn becomes a mighty oak tree?" he asked.

"How?"

"The little nut just holds his ground," chuckled Tim.

"I'll have to tell the folks that one."

"I've a serious question for you. At school I heard that King David has a hole in his cheek but none of the kids know why. Is it true?"

"Some say a bushwhacker shot him and it locked his jaw. He had to have three top and three bottom teeth pulled in order to be able to eat. Another story has it that he got typhoid at fifteen and the Doc gave him mercurial chloride and you just can't eat certain food when you take it. He talked his three-year-old sister into sneaking him a pickle from a barrel under the house. He bit down on it, got lockjaw, and could never open his mouth again. Since he couldn't open his mouth to eat or speak, a hole had to be cut in his cheek."

"Wow! You just about made me lose my taste for pickles."

About that time, they heard a man cry out very close to where they were.

"That's it! That's it!" Tim said. "That's what I heard earlier this morning."

"C'mon, we can tie up our horses and slip up the side of the hill where we can see what's going on. Don't make a sound."

The boys crept quietly up the hillside. They saw a man held on a table by two other men while a third man beat the culprit's feet with a cane stick.

The man was crying, "I'm sorry, I won't do it again! Please don't hit me again!" After several more blows, the beating stopped and the officials led the limping man to a nearby shed. Without a word, Tim and Otto crept back down to their horses, mounted up, and rode towards the Smith farm.

Finally, Otto broke the silence.

"You know, not all of the suffering in this world is caused by punishment for crimes, right? Some things happen just because of pure meanness. Like back a few years ago, when some boys caught a dog near the store in Everett, poured turpentine on him, and tied tin cans to him. The dog streaked home yelping like crazy. His owner thought he'd gone mad and shot him—his own dog."

"That's bad. I better keep a close eye on Jack and Pumpkin. I sure don't want anything like that happening to them. With all the mean tricks in the world, it's good to know we've got a good fishing hole. Maybe next time we'll have time to fish."

"You're right about that! Speaking of time…." Otto looked at the position of the sun. "We should be heading back for dinner."

The boys heard Betty's screams before they even reached the yard and instinctively urged Thunder and Lightning into a gallop. They charged past the house and tool shed in time to see her fly out the door of the chicken house. Tim and Otto ran toward her just as Mrs. Smith jumped from the back porch to see what had happened.

"Gracious, Betty! What's gotten into you? Are you hurt?" she cried.

"I was gathering the eggs and one of the hens was sitting on her nest, so I reached under her to check for eggs and when I did, when I did, I felt this slimy thing instead! There's a huge black snake curled up under her! It scared me to death as you can tell. It's that nest right over there!"

Tim's and Mrs. Smith's eyes widened in alarm; only Otto remained calm. "It's probably just a black snake after the eggs. Regular black snakes aren't poisonous like black water moccasins which usually stay close to, well, water."

He took a stick and gently raised the hen and grabbed the black snake behind the head. With a smaller stick he pried open the snake's mouth and showed the Smiths the horseshoe shaped row of teeth.

"See, if this snake was a poisonous snake, it would have two fangs. I'll take it far out in the pasture where it can find some mice to eat instead of your eggs."

"Oh thank you! Thank you, Otto." Betty said, "It's great to have a friend who knows his snakes. From now on when I gather the eggs, I'll take a stick and check under the hens first to make sure there are no snakes there."

"You're welcome, Betty," Otto stammered, surprised to feel his cheeks get hot. "I'm just glad you're O.K."

Chapter 8—Dressing Chickens and a Big Storm

"Mae, Honey, how's roast chicken sound for dinner tonight?" asked Mr. Smith at breakfast.

"Roast chicken? You know perfectly well what we've got in the cooler and there's certainly…."

"Now, Honey, settle down." he chuckled. "Kids, today's your lucky day. I'm going to teach you how to ready a chicken for your mother."

"Really, Dad? When do we start?" chimed Tim eagerly.

"The second batch of young roosters we caponized are now big enough to eat, so as soon as you've finished the breakfast dishes, we'll head out to the yard."

Betty, not as sure about this new responsibility as her brother, lingered a little longer than usual over the sink. "Betty-Boo? Is it the chicken?" Mrs. Smith inquired, taking the towel from her daughter's hand.

"I suppose it is. We'll have to kill it? Right there in the yard?"

"Honey, you know we live on what we grow or kill. We always have."

"Not always. You used to get your chicken from Grandma!"

"And where do you think she got our chicken? It's part of life, Sweetheart. Now go on out there and spend some time with your father and brother."

"There are several ways to kill a chicken…." She heard her father say as she trudged down the porch steps. With a quick nod that told her he understood her anxiety, he went on, "We can lay the chicken's head across a tree stump and cut the head off with an ax like people do the Thanksgiving Turkey. Or we can take the chicken by the neck and whirl it round and round until its

49

head comes off." Tim gulped. "...*Whirl it round and round till its head comes off?*" He tried to look grown up as he refocused on his father. "I prefer to take my foot and step on its head while holding onto its feet. Then I pull until his head comes off. It will jump around for awhile."

"How long's a while Daddy?" Betty couldn't keep the terror from creeping into her voice.

"About two or three minutes, Betty-Boo. You take the chicken, scald him; pluck off the feathers and then take him to where you've built a fire and rotate it over the flames until you've singed off all the pinfeathers. Now, let me show you how to use this heavy wire to grab one of our juicy capons by the leg, and then you two can go and make a fire."

Mr. Smith caught one, and in just a few seconds the headless capon was jumping around in the yard. They took him into the kitchen, plunged him into a pan of scalding water, and Mrs. Smith helped them pluck off handfuls of feathers. Then they took the capon outside where they had built a fire. Within minutes they were singeing off the remaining pinfeathers over the open flames. Betty turned to Tim, "Let's make a deal. From now on, if you'll behead the chickens and help me with the fire, I'll help Mom clean and cook them."

Tim eagerly agreed, "It's a deal. This is almost as easy as dressing fish or squirrels."

That evening when the capon was served for supper, everyone thought it was one of the best they'd ever tasted. Even Betty.

Their high spirits took a turn though when Mr. Smith went to make his after-supper check on the barn. Clouds threatened to the west, punctuated by occasional flashes of lightning. It looked like they could expect a storm during the night.

"If that storm is as bad as it looks from here, we'll need to go to the storm cellar sometime during the night," cautioned Mr. Smith. "When you kids go to bed this evening, lay your clothes where you can find them and have a jacket or a quilt to put over your head. We'll need to go in a hurry when the time comes."

Sure enough, about midnight the wind started to howl so hard it shook the house. As the lightning began to light up the yard, Mr. Smith lit the kerosene lantern and called out, "Hurry kids, put on your clothes, grab your jackets, and head to the cellar!"

The rain and hail sounded like milk buckets falling on the tin roof of the back porch as they gathered in the kitchen near the door which led to the cellar. "Who knew rain could hurt?" thought Betty as they raced towards the shelter. Safely inside with the door shut overhead, everyone felt secure amid stored fruits and vegetables.

"I'm glad there's a hole in the tool shed where Jack and Pumpkin can get out of the storm," Tim said.

"Yes, and a barn where Blaze is protected," added Betty.

Mr. Smith said, "It would be nice if all of our animals could be inside on a night like this but it just isn't possible. Let's hope none of them get struck by lightning. This is a bad storm. You can tell how far away a storm is by the amount of time between the bolt of lightning and the noise of the thunder. Tonight the thunder and lightning are so close together, the storm must be passing directly over us."

Once the rain settled into a gentle tapping on the door, Mr. Smith looked outside to check on the storm. After a brief prayer, he gave the all-clear.

"A time or two I was afraid that wind was going to tip our house over! I'm really glad the Monroes left the piano. If it hadn't been in the southwest corner of our house, it might have been blown over!" Remembering that his dad had once told him that several horses and head of cattle were killed each year by lightning strikes, Tim said, "I wonder if any of our animals got struck by any of the lightning bolts."

"I think they're probably just fine, but Son, that's good thinking. You come with me to check on them. Since it's already Saturday, I say we stay in bed an hour longer than usual—the cows won't want to be milked so soon anyway after this storm. Girls, you head on into the house now and snuggle back into bed."

Chapter 9—Snake Bite

Owens Creek was still rising from the summer rains. The hedge fence that encircled the Smith's eighty acres whipped back and forth in the crisp wind as a slight drizzle filled the air. Tim hoped it would clear off by the time he finished his chores, since he and Otto knew this was the time when the fish would be biting. Tim already had a good supply of earthworms, and Otto planned to bring some dough balls to entice the carp.

By the time Tim finished, Otto galloped up on Lightning.

"You about ready? We can cut our fishing poles when we get there," Otto said. Both the boys carried razor-sharp hunting knives.

"Don't worry about meat for supper, Mrs. Smith. Tim and I will bring back plenty of fish."

Betty stuck her head out the back door. "We can cook all you guys can catch," she said as she smiled at Otto. Mrs. Smith joined her and looked at Otto.

"Would you like to eat supper with us this evening?"

"I'd like that. I'm sure it will be O.K., but let me call and check with Mom. Tim will need someone to help him clean all those fish we're gonna catch."

Tim grabbed his fishing line, bait, lunch, and water jug. He put everything into two bags, tied them together, and tossed them over Thunder's shoulders as he called out to his mother, "Tell Dad I'll be home in time to do my part of the chores."

"Thanks, honey, I'll let your dad know. And Otto, why don't I call your mom and tell her I've invited you to stay for supper."

"Thanks Mrs. Smith! That'd be great." So the boys mounted up and off they went.

The road was muddy and slick as they headed for the best fishing area of Owens Creek.

On the way, they saw squirrels, turtledoves, and rabbits, and they often heard the "Ah Bob White" whistle of the quail. As they rounded a bend in the road, Tim pointed.

"Look, there's a mother skunk crossing the road with four little ones following her! Your dad will be glad to know more skunks are in this neck of the woods. That should help his fur trading business."

"That's a pretty sight, but several skunks were found dead a few days ago and we're afraid they may be catching some disease. There doesn't seem to be any shortage of rabbits this year though. Be ready to hang on if our horses shy when a rabbit jumps out unexpectedly from the brush along the side of the road. By the way, do you have a joke for us today?"

"Sure. Do you know what causes a flood?"

"No. What?"

"A flood happens when a river gets too big for its bridges."

"I can't argue with that," Otto said.

"And do you know why a dog is such a friendly animal?"

"No, why?"

"Because he wags his tail instead of his tongue."

"I can't argue with that either."

When they began to go down into Owens Creek, Otto suggested they start near the small waterfall. The spot not only had good fishing but also boasted a cave that would protect them from any sudden showers.

The boys slipped halters on their horses so they could graze, and cut a couple of fishing poles.

"We're in luck," said Otto. "It looks like the creek is still rising and the fish will be looking for food that washes in."

Tim baited his hook with a fat juicy earthworm and moved his line up and down just beneath the waterfall. Suddenly he felt a tug at the other end of the line, and he immediately set the hook in the fish's mouth by giving the line a quick jerk. He pulled a foot-long bullhead catfish out of the water. Definitely a keeper; it soon dangled from a stringer which he tossed into the water and anchored to the bank. By this time Otto had cast a dough ball in the pool just below the waterfalls.

"I've got a bite too." He pulled in a carp about twice as long as the fish Tim had caught.

"Are carp good to eat?" Tim asked. "I've never had one before."

"Carps are more boney than catfish but I like 'em."

Each boy caught another couple of fish before the biting slowed down.

"I'm going down stream a little way to a deeper hole." said Otto. "Call me if you need anything."

"Sure," said Tim, "And give me a yell if I can help you."

Next, Tim caught a sun perch about the size of the palm of his hand, and then a sucker. He knew the small sucker would be too bony to eat, so he threw it back. As he was fishing, he caught a glimpse of something orange and brown under a tuff of grass. Figuring it might be a colorful toad or tree frog of some kind, he decided to catch it and surprise Otto.

Tim quickly wedged his fishing pole in the rocks and snuck up on the clump of grass. As he took his left hand and lifted up the tuff of grass, he took his right hand and grabbed at the patch of orange and brown.

"Ouch! Help!" he cried out. He had grabbed a snake! It was about eight inches long and flipped its head around and bit Tim between the thumb and forefinger of his left hand.

He cried out as loudly as he could, "Otto, come quick! I've been bitten by a snake!"

Otto jabbed his fishing pole in the soft bank and ran to Tim. When he saw the snake clinging to Tim's hand, Otto whipped out his hunting knife and quickly cut off its head and removed it from Tim's hand.

"Be as calm as you can", Otto said. "That's a copperhead. See those two fang marks on your hand? A poisonous snake makes two fang marks. If the snake was a nonpoisonous one, the teeth marks would be in a horseshoe shape."

"Will I die?" Tim asked.

"I don't think so."

"You don't think so? Otto!"

"Relax, a lot of people get bitten by copperheads but very few die."

"Whew! That's a relief. That was a dumb thing I did. I was just going to surprise you with what I thought was a toad or tree frog. Guess we both got surprised by this snake."

Otto poured water from Tim's water jug on the bite and took his clean handkerchief and tied it over the fang marks.

"Try to hold your hand and arm as still as possible. I'll help you up on Thunder. We need to get you over to Everett to see Dr. Brown right now. I'll come back later and pick up the fish."

Otto wrapped the snake head in Tim's handkerchief and stuck it in his pocket so he could show the doctor.

"Hey Otto? I'm kind of scared. I've never been bit by a poisonous snake before and it sort of stings."

"You may get a little sleepy but stay awake. Give me your foot and I will hoist you up on Thunder."

The boys, side by side, rode the three miles to the doctor's office in the fastest trot they could. Thunder and Lightning seemed to sense they were in a hurry. Otto tried to keep Tim awake, keeping up a constant stream of conversation. "The poisonous snakes we have around here are rattlesnakes, copperheads, and cottonmouth water moccasins, so Doc treats a lot of snakebites. I've had a couple, and once he treated me when I had a bad case of poison ivy."

Tim said, "I should have been more careful."

The boys arrived at Dr. Brown's office in less than an hour.

"That's a copperhead, alright," he confirmed as he cleaned and treated the wound. "You're going to be O.K., Tim, but your hand will be sore and you'll need to take it easy for a few days. Use some of this salve and put a clean bandage on it each day. Send word if you have any trouble."

Tim called home and told his mom what had happened. Then Dr. Brown took the phone and convinced her that Tim would be fine and that they could pay him later. Tim thanked the doctor, and the boys headed out the door.

"I'm sure glad we have a doctor here or I might have been a goner! And I'm also glad I have a good friend like you, because you knew what to do. Thanks, Otto!"

"After we get back to your house, I'll ride back over to Owens Creek and get our fish, and then head back to your place. I'll help with the milking." When they arrived at Tim's house, Mrs. Smith rushed from the porch where she'd been waiting.

"Thank the Lord you are both safe. It sounds like you did exactly the right thing. Otto, we're so grateful!"

Everybody insisted that Tim go in and lie down so he could recover from the snake bite more quickly. Tim laid his head back on the pillow and prayed silently,

"Thank you, God, for friends like Otto, Dr. Brown, and my family. Without them I could have died today. I'll try to be more careful next time, and some day perhaps *I can help someone who gets into trouble."*

Soon he was fast asleep and woke up when his Dad gently shook him and said, "Supper's ready; let's see how the fish and cornbread taste and be thankful everything today turned out for the best."

Tim said, "Yes, and from now on I will not reach down and pick up critters out of the grass. I don't care how colorful they are!"

Chapter 10—Kidnapped

Otto came back to the Smiths' house the next evening to help with the chores while Tim continued to recover, which gave Mr. Smith another chance to thank him.

"I'm glad to do it, Mr. Smith. What are friends for? I have lots of friends, and Tim is one of my best friends. Hey, tomorrow I plan to set some traps near the creek close to the prairie where the Indians live. Last week, Tim and I saw some raccoon, opossum, and skunk tracks near that part of Owens Creek."

"I heard there used to be lots of stealing between the Prairie people and the Amarugians."

"There was. My parents told me that when some Prairie people invaded Amarugia, they captured the King and held him prisoner, hoping to get a heavy ransom. The Kingdom refused to pay the ransom, and the King got some kind of disease and died. The council placed Owens II in his place and things went back to being peaceful."

"That sounds sort of scary. I'm glad things have remained quiet though!"

Otto and Mr. Smith finished up the milking, turned the cows out to pasture, separated the cream from the milk, and washed the containers before joining the rest of the Smiths for supper.

When they'd finished, Otto thanked Mrs. Smith and added, "Since I'm planning to set traps tomorrow, I may be a little late getting back to help with the milking tomorrow evening." He made his goodbyes and headed back home.

The next morning, at breakfast, Otto told his dad he would be setting out some traps in a new place.

"I wish I could go with you, but I have some furs coming from the South Fork area and I need to be at the Post to take care of business."

After doing his chores around the house, Otto put his traps into a sack and gave Lightning the secret signal of two clicks and a whistle. He'd taught Lightning to buck off anybody, including himself, who didn't use this signal before mounting. He put Lightning into a quick trot west toward Owens Creek. He followed the creek for approximately a half mile southwest where he'd previously seen tracks. He took the bridle off and put a halter on Lightning so he could graze. Otto then went about the work of finding the best places to set his traps. He set several traps but as he bent over to set and camouflage another, he heard something whistle through the air and make a thud as it hit the tree trunk just above his head. He looked up and saw an arrow sticking there. Looking around, he saw several Indians standing in a circle with bows drawn and arrows pointed directly at him. One addressed him.

"Throw hunting knife on ground and put your hands in air!"

Otto threw his knife on the ground and while raising his hands asked, "Why? Have I done something wrong?" The Indians didn't answer. The leader said to one of the other Indians, "Get pony." Then he pointed at Otto and said, "You follow pony." Otto knew the unwritten "first come, first serve" rule in the trapping business, but he'd not seen any signs forbidding trapping on the east side of Owens Creek. As far as he knew, he'd done nothing wrong.

Lightning tossed his head and snorted when the stranger picked up the rope but when he saw Otto, he followed the Indian peacefully. As they were walking along, the Indians started talking in their tribal Osage language. They didn't know that Otto's mother had taught him the language when he was young and that he understood what they were saying. He heard them say they had seen this stallion and they knew he could run as fast as the wind and that the tribe wanted to breed him with their ponies. They also discussed the possibility of some ransom money, because they knew his father was a fur trader.

They walked about four miles down a trail until they came to the Indian village. Once there, they put Otto into a small one-room shack and barred the door. Two guards sat just outside and he overheard one of them say that the chief's son would want to be the first to ride the stallion. Otto could see through the solitary tiny window that they'd put Lightning in a corral and that a boy about his own age was getting ready to ride him.

"He must be the Chief's son," Otto thought. *"He's in for a big surprise."*

Sure enough, as soon as the young Indian mounted Lightning, the stallion bucked him off. The boy jumped up, brushed himself off and had some of the others hold the reins as he mounted the second time. Again Lightning threw him off. After hitting the ground the second time, he looked around at those crowding around the corral, and asked, "Which one of you thinks he can ride this wild bucking bronco?"

Three hands went up at once, but it wasn't long before all three ended up on the ground. Then one of the older Indians said, "We leave pony in the corral tonight, and by tomorrow he may let us ride."

Otto was very proud of Lightning for putting into practice what he'd been taught, but as it began to get dark, he began to wonder what their fate would be.

The Smiths, in the meantime had become anxious about Otto's whereabouts. He'd said that he might be a little late getting back from setting out his traps, but Mr. Smith had almost finished the chores and still no Otto. Mr. Smith called the Swartzs' home and told them Otto hadn't shown up at their house to help with the chores.

Mr. Swartz hurried over and, together with Mr. Smith, decided to take a couple of lanterns and check the area where Otto said he'd planned to set some traps. Walking, so they would not make as much noise, they came to a place where they found some traps and many footprints—from shoes and moccasins—as well as pony tracks.

"Oh, no! Indians must have kidnapped Otto and Lightning!" After thinking what might be best to do, Mr. Swartz ruefully added, "We'd better wait until morning or we may do more harm than good if we go into unfamiliar territory. We might trigger a fight and be outnumbered. I suspect all this has something to do with Lightning. I've heard more than a few customers say they'd like to have a stallion like him."

"Why don't we get an early start around daylight tomorrow?" Mr. Smith offered. "We can leave word with our wives where we're headed just in case we get captured. Then, if we're not back by a certain time, they can tell King David and he can send help. In the meantime, we'll pray that this will have a good outcome."

They backtracked until they reached the crossroad, where they shook hands and went to tell their families about the plans for tomorrow.

Back at the shack, a guard passed a plate of deer meat, corn on the cob, and some water through a slot at the bottom of the little window. As he looked out this window, Otto saw one of the Indians carry a bucket of water and put some hay out for Lightning. The shack had a deer-hide on the floor and he figured he should try getting some rest. He knew his dad would come looking for him as soon as it was daylight. He was glad he had told both his dad and Mr. Smith the general area where he planned to set the traps, and he prayed to the Lord as he tried to think of how he might escape.

He moved the stool over to the door where he could hear the Indian guards talking to each other.

"That must be a one-man horse. He only lets the owner ride him. Tomorrow morning, our chief says he will have us bring boy to the corral and make him teach the chief's son how to ride this bucking stallion."

Otto immediately got an idea.

"I'll tell the Chief I need to ride my pony around the track a few times to let him warm up. They probably don't know he is also a jumping stallion. After I ride him around the corral twice, I will steer him straight for that section of the corral near the trail. Lightning can easily jump that. When we hit the road, we will be around the bend before they can stop us."

Then he prayed, *"If you'll help me Lord, I promise to be a better follower of You."*

Otto finally fell off to sleep and woke up early the next morning when he heard the guard shoving his breakfast, consisting of two hard boiled eggs and Indian bread, through the little opening.

"Hurry up; eat, boy. Our chief want see you at corral right after breakfast."

Otto gulped down the food and put the empty plate back in the opening. He could see a crowd of Indians lined up all the way around the corral and Lightning was swishing his tail, tossing his head, and snorting. He wouldn't let any of the Indians get close to him. The guards came to lead Otto down to the corral. The chief waited at the gate with his son.

"We want you show us how to ride pony!"

"O.K., I'll show you," Otto said. He walked over to Lightning, who whinnied and neighed with a low contented sound as Otto patted him on the neck. Otto then put a bridle on him and led him out to the center of the corral. He patted Lightning once more on the neck and scratched Lightning's left ear. As he did so, he gave too clicks and a short whistle. The sounds were so soft the Indians could not hear them. Otto then tossed his right leg over Lightning as he sprang from the ground. He rode Lightning around the corral the first time in a trot. The second time around, he put him into his jumping stride. When they were about halfway around, Otto headed Lightning straight for the section of the corral next to the trail. They sailed over the fence and hit the ground at a gallop, and within a few seconds they were around the bend and out of sight! As Lightning galloped as fast as he could, Otto patted him on the shoulder, "Good boy, Lightning, I knew you could do it!" hooted Otto. Otto and Lightning stayed ahead of the Indian arrows. They were home in a short time where his Mother and Dovie welcomed him with open arms and tears of gratitude.

"Thank heavens you're safe!" she cried. "Your dad and Mr. Smith have been out looking for you. They should be here in a few minutes."

Before long they saw the men running up the road toward the house. Mr. Swartz ran up to Otto. He gave him a big hug as tears filled his eyes.

"Thank the Lord you're safe! At first when I saw Lightning alone in that corral, I was afraid they might have killed you for your pony. We were watching from a nearby hilltop and saw you being led to the corral. Boy was I relieved! I didn't know what you were going to do, but I knew you and Lightning would think of something. When you jumped that fence, we knew you'd beat us home. I'm proud of you, Son. A person who uses good judgment like that will make us Amarugians a good King some day."

"I didn't feel my life was in danger after I overheard the Indians talking. They were more interested in Lightning than they were in me. Some of them had seen how fast Lightning runs, and they want to breed him with their ponies. Do you think we could work out a plan where they could trade furs for the breeding fee?"

"Let me sleep on it, son. You may have a good idea there. We'll see. It would give us more income and help our relations with the Indians."

That evening Lightning got an extra serving of oats, corn, and hay, and Otto slept like a baby after he had thanked the Lord for watching over them.

Chapter 11—Peace Plan

Otto and Lightning's escape stirred up a lot of excitement back at the Indian village. Amazed at the pony's jumping ability, several of the children made sketches on pieces of bark. One even drew wings on his because he had never seen a pony jump that high. Another drew a halo over his brown and white pony.

Chief Wise Owl, his fifteen year old son, Bold Eagle, and two other leaders of the tribe met to decide what to do. They knew it would be dangerous to ride into the Kingdom of Amarugia, especially after hearing about the painful bastinado punishment King David Wilson gave those guilty of serious crimes.

"Why not have two or three of us ride to the trading post tomorrow morning and just tell the truth," suggested one of the older Indians. "We want to have our ponies bred by the brown and white stallion but kidnapping him was a big mistake. Let's tell them that we're sorry and that it won't happen again, and that we will pay regular breeding fees with the furs we deliver."

"I'll give back the boy's hunting knife to show we mean peace," Bold Eagle offered. "I can have several pelts ready by tomorrow morning, and why don't we take the drawings to show how much we like the great stallion?"

Meanwhile back in Amarugia, Tim and his dad rode over to Otto's house. They found Otto and Lightning resting up from all the excitement. Their fathers were discussing what action they should take concerning the kidnapping.

"I think I know what the problem is," Tim heard Mr. Swartz saying. "We need to have an understanding with the Indians about the trapping boundaries in the Owens Creek area. This 'first come, first serve' idea isn't working because it's impossible to prove who had the idea to trap there first. Why don't we get an agreement that we will trap on this side of Owens Creek and they can trap on the other side?"

"That should work," Mr. Smith agreed.

"Let's offer to exchange stud fees with them for the value of the pelts they bring in. They really don't have much money and this way it will help both sides," added Otto.

The men agreed.

"Let's sleep on it tonight, son, and see if we hear anything from them tomorrow. You know, if this plan works," he smiled, "It just may help us to answer the age-old question— 'What's that have to do with the price of a fur cap in Amarugia?'" They all chuckled.

Mr. Smith turned to Otto and said, "Thanks for your help while Tim's hand was healing. Tim and I will stop by your store after we get the morning chores done, just in case the Indians try to contact you."

Tim turned to Otto and said, "Tomorrow, I want to hear all about what happened to you in the Indian village." Otto agreed, and the boys said goodnight.

The next morning, two of the older Indians and Bold Eagle, the chief's son, approached the Fur Trading Post. One of their ponies dripped raccoon hides, opossum pelts, and a couple of wolf hides. Another carried some dried venison and a couple of sacks of Indian corn. Bold Eagle personally held onto the sketches and Otto's hunting knife.

As planned, the Smiths and Swartzs' were already there when the Indians rode up and tied their ponies to the hitching rack. The older Indians entered first. One introduced himself as Wise Hawk and the other said his name was Evening Shade. Wise Hawk apologized, "We sorry for what happened. We want you and your son to have these pelts as presents, and we promise not to kidnap him again." Evening Shade continued, "Your pony is a great pony and your son is a great son! We want to make peace. We'll bring in presents, and then we'll go." Karl inspected the pelts and saw they were in excellent condition. He noticed they seemed sorry for what they had done, not just sorry they got caught. Bold Eagle gave Otto back his hunting knife and said he was sorry he took it. He then pulled several pieces of bark out of his saddle bags. Everyone was amazed at the drawings of Lightning and Otto jumping over the fence. Mr. Swartz invited everyone to sit down.

"We accept your apologies and your gifts. Let's see what we can work out. To avoid future trouble with the trapping boundaries, let's agree that you can have all the pelts you trap on the west side of Owens Creek, and we will keep all the pelts we trap on the east side. Also, you're clearly interested in having your ponies bred by Lightning. We'd be willing to exchange pelts for breeding fees. Take this idea back to your chief, and tomorrow let us know if you agree."

The three Indians huddled together and spoke a few words. Wise Hawk responded. "This we do and we'll be back tomorrow with answer." The next morning the Indians returned as promised. They'd brought some of the finest pelts Mr. Swartz had ever seen. While they discussed and signed the agreement, Otto and Bold Eagle spoke, and discovered they knew some of the same people.

"I think Bold Eagle and I are going to become friends," Otto said after the Indians left. "He and I are about the same age and have a lot in common. Bold Eagle will be a good friend to have when I become King, but I'm not going to tell him about the signal I give Lightning before I ride him, nor am I going to tell him I understand his language, at least not yet!" Everyone agreed that was a good idea.

Amarugia Highlands View from the Chris Christiansen Hill
or Mound with Prairie Lands in the Distance
October 12, 1958

Shown in the foreground is the Chris Christiansen home where
Jesse James once stayed overnight with the Wilson Davenport
family from whom Christiansens bought the house and farm.

Photograph by Donald Lewis Osborn.

Chapter 12 — Harvest Time

Another important job on the farm was to prepare for the winter months by getting enough hay in the barn. There were hay stacks left out in the fields after the wheat and oat harvest but the lespedeza, timothy, and alfalfa hay needed to be cut and carried to the barn.

Mr. Smith told Betty and Tim that he would need their help on Saturday to bring the hay from the field and put it into the hayloft of the barn. Also, the grandparents came to help.

"I've cut the hay and have it in piles so we can put it on our hay frame wagons and haul it to the barn. Betty, I'll need you to drive the hay frame and Tim and Otto will toss it up to you and Grandpa. While you are on your way to the barn, the boys will load up the other hay frame for you to pick up when you return. When you get to the barn, we have old Belle hooked up to a rope which goes through the barn to a big fork, which is let down to the hay frame, and Grandpa Smith will clamp the fork around a bunch of hay. Then your mom will lead Belle forward and the clamp loaded with the glob of hay will be pulled into the barn loft by pulleys where I will be. As soon as the load of hay rides along the trolley to where I want it dumped, I will pull the trip rope and the clamp will release the hay. Then I will take my pitchfork and arrange the hay where it should go in the loft. It's kind of hard to explain in words but just as soon as you see it in action, it will seem real simple."

"Are there any bull nettles in the hay?" Betty wanted to know.

"Yes, a few. But like they say, 'The tail always goes with the hide;' we just have to grin and bear it, even with the bull nettles." Tim wanted to know which field they would do first, and Mr. Smith answered, "The alfalfa, then the timothy field, and finally the lespedeza."

69

"Let's all try to get a good night's sleep because it will be hard work tomorrow, but in another couple of weekends we'll have all the hay we'll need this winter in a safe place in the barn. Then in a few weeks it'll be time to shuck corn."

It seemed that there was no end to jobs to do on the farm, but it was very interesting, especially since this was their first time to do many of those tasks.

That Saturday as Otto arrived to help with the haying, Tim told him, "I'm sure glad you all don't have a big farm to keep up with so my dad can hire you part time to help us when we have big jobs to get done."

"I enjoy it, too. Especially since the fur business has been slow this year. It gives me a little spending money, too. We have only thirty acres of pasture land, but that's enough for Lightning and our three other ponies."

Everything went fine on Saturday morning. Betty hauled several loads of alfalfa hay to the barn and when she arrived at the barn, Grandpa Smith clamped the big metal clamp around as much hay as it could hold. Then Mrs. Smith led Belle straight ahead as she pulled the rope which ran on pulleys through the barn and lifted the big glob of hay into the barn. When it arrived over the spot where Mr. Smith wanted it, he pulled the trigger and the clamp dropped the hay. Then he took his pitchfork and spread it where it should go in the hay loft. This procedure was repeated over and over all morning long until all the alfalfa had been put into the barn. By noon time, everyone was hungry. Grandma Smith had lunch prepared, and by one o'clock they were ready to bring the timothy hay into the barn. They knew that the horses loved timothy hay and they seemed to thrive on it during the winter months.

When Betty was bringing in her second load of loose hay, she didn't see the big rock in her path. When the right front wheel of the wagon ran over it, the load of hay tipped over and all the hay covered her. She screamed as she disappeared under all that hay. Grandpa was holding onto the back of the wagon.

Grandpa and Mrs. Smith saw what had happened and Grandpa told Mrs. Smith to grab the bridle of the nearest horse and he started digging into the pile of hay to find Betty. She was O.K. and was still holding tightly to the reins. Mr. Smith ran out of the barn and shouted, "What happened? Betty, are you O.K.?"

Betty brushed herself off and smiled as she said, "Yes, I'm O.K. Just shook up a bit. I guess I'm initiated as a farmer now."

They loaded the hay back onto the wagon and led the horses to where the hay was to be unloaded. Betty went on to the house to wash up since it was time for dinner.

Grandma Smith had prepared dinner, and she came to the front porch and called out, "Everybody wash up for dinner; come and get it!"

Mr. Smith turned in the direction of the fields and with a shrill whistle let Otto and Tim know that it was dinner time. They unhooked the horses, watered them at the pond, put them in their stalls, and gave them some timothy hay and oats.

When they reached the house, Tim asked, "Did something happen? We heard something which sounded like a scream but couldn't figure out what had happened."

"It was me," Betty said, "I got turned over by a fairly good-sized rock and it dumped the hay all over me when we tipped over."

"Were you hurt?" Otto wanted to know.

"No, just my feelings, I guess. It happened so fast, it scared me and I screamed. It seems like I always scream when I get frightened."

The boys said they were glad she wasn't injured, and Otto said he was sorry he was out in the field and wasn't able to help.

"That's O.K., Otto, I know you both would have helped if you were here," Betty said with a smile. Grandma Smith was sure a good cook and although they all felt like taking a nap after dinner, they headed back out to the barn and fields to finish the job.

After the hay was all put into the barn, the next job was shucking corn. One Saturday, Mr. Smith and Tim put the backboard on the right side of the wagon so they could toss the shucked ears of corn against the backboard and the ears would fall into the wagon. The corn crop was good, and when the wagon got full of those ears of yellow corn, it looked like a wagon full of gold.

"I can just see the calves I'm feeding to sell and to butcher, getting fat on all this beautiful corn," observed Tim.

"Do you know that they even have corn shucking contests in some parts of the country?" Mr. Smith said.

"No, I didn't know that, but I'll bet it's fun if a guy gets good enough at it. At the rate I'm going, I'll be grown and then some before I'm fast enough to enter any contest."

"Be sure and keep your gloves on and use that husking tool I gave you, and the soreness in your wrists will not be as noticeable in a few days."

Finally, the corn was all brought into the corn crib, and another big job was finished in preparation for the winter months.

Chapter 13 — Doves, Chaff, and Tobacco

All the crops were growing and maturing, and the morning grass sparkled with dew. Still hoping to catch some fish, the boys were headed to Owens Creek. Tim turned to Otto, "So tell me about the dove hunt coming up next week. I've never been to one. What's it like?"

"People will come from as far away as Kansas City and boy, will they be trigger happy."

Tim raised a questioning eyebrow.

"Some of them will shoot at anything that moves. Turtledoves are fast flyers and it's hard to hit them in flight."

"Don't they mostly eat insects and weed seeds on the ground? Why not just shoot 'em like rabbits?" asked Tim.

Otto gave Tim a stern look. "Do you really think it's fair to shoot them while they eat?"

Tim looked ashamed and shook his head. Otto, not wanting to embarrass his friend any further, continued. "Everyone knows they coo, but if you haven't been to a dove hunt, I bet you haven't heard them take off. It sounds like a bunch of scared chickens scattering in every which direction."

"You plan to hunt?"

"I don't think so. I like eating them, but they're so small it takes forever to shoot enough to make a meal. I'll tell you this though. I'm keeping Lightning in the barn as much as I can next week. I sure wouldn't want one of those trigger happy visitors hitting him by accident. I'll need to help Dad at the Trading Post most of the week since there will be so many strangers in the area. They really buy a lot of ammunition and our coonskin caps."

"I'm going to keep Thunder in the barn, too. Dad wants me to help repair our horses' harness. He's taught me how to use brads to splice the broken pieces of leather together."

Tim continued, "We'll start harvesting our grain crops soon. Dad said one of our neighbors has a combine which cuts and ties the grain into bundles, and then we put 10 or 12 of these bundles together and make what is called a shock. All those shocks of grain look like an Indian village scattered all over the field. This also keeps the heads of the grain off the ground until our time for thrashing comes up. Another neighbor has a big thrashing machine, and he goes from farm to farm as we all help one another bring in the crops. Dad says I can be water boy this year."

Otto liked to hear Tim tell about his new experiences on the farm.

"I told your dad the other day I'd be glad to help. The last three years I've followed the thrashing crews. One year I pitched bundles from the shocks to the wagons. The next year I drove one of the wagons which picked up the bundles and I pitched them off into the thrashing machine and then last year I drove one of the grain wagons which caught the grain and then I hauled it to the barn where I scooped the wheat and oats into one of the grain bins. I always learn something from listening to the guys talk as they work. All the moms and older daughters get together to cook dinner for the thrashing crews. Their food is great, too, and a guy really gets in good shape with all that pitching of bundles and shoveling of grain!"

"Mom and Betty are planning to make a bunch of different pies."

"Great! You know I love their cooking!"

"Do you ever find any animals under the shocks of grain?"

"If they've been there for several days you may find all sorts of stuff—snakes, rabbits, mice, rats, terrapins, and no telling what else. That's part of what makes it exciting. You'll have to bear up under the bull nettles though. They get in your clothes and stick to your skin and they itch like the dickens."

74

"I'll be sure to keep an eye out for those!" said Tim earnestly.

The boys continued their ride amid the cooing of the turtle-doves, interrupted only by the occasional flinching of Lightning and Thunder when the startled doves would fly off their nests.

As the Amarugia Dove Hunt got underway, the pelt business all but ground to a halt at the Fur Trading Post. Too afraid to check their traps with trigger happy visiting hunters, many of whom were drinking, folks came into the Post to share tales of near misses and stray bullets. Sales of coonskin caps, moccasins, and gun shells picked up though, and business was good.

Tim and Betty worked extra hard in getting all their chores done at home so they could help the Swartz family at their store. Otto and Betty always seemed to be close enough to each other during the slack times to visit. Otto explained everything in the trading post to Betty and she was a quick learner and everyone could see they worked well as a team. Otto worked so fast that occasionally he would gently bump up against Betty or his hand would touch her arm. Often she would pat him on the back as soon as the customer left when they had a good sale.

On the morning that the thrashing season began, Tim saddled up Thunder, gathered four gallon water jugs, and wrapped them with gunnysacks. He filled the jugs with fresh water and then poured some over the sacks to keep the jugs cool. Two of the jugs he left under a shade tree near the field of wheat. He tied one jug on each side of Thunder's saddle and set out for the fields. The big thrashing machine had arrived the previous afternoon and everything was ready to go. Several neighbors had brought their teams and hay frames, and even Grandpa Smith came out from Archie to help. Otto had his pitchfork and was already pitching bundles of wheat on a wagon. As the sun became a blazing ball of fire in the sky the workers loaded bundle after bundle of wheat onto the wagons. When a wagon was loaded, the driver would pull it alongside the big thrashing machine and pitch in the bundles on a conveyer belt where it was taken and the husks were thrashed off. As the machinery roared, a steady stream of wheat poured out a metal sleeve into the grain wagon, and the chaff blew out another spout. When the wagon was full, the grain was taken to the barn where it was stored. Tim did his best to see to their thirst. He couldn't believe how many trips he had to make to refill his jugs!

In the meantime, mothers and daughters bustled in the Smith kitchen, preparing fried chicken, mashed potatoes, vegetables, and gallons of ice tea. The younger girls helped set out the dozens of cakes, pies, and cookies baked over the weekend for just this occasion. When Mrs. Smith rang the dinner bell, the men closest to the house waved their arms to signal those who were near the noisy thrashing machine to shut it down for dinner. A line of men and boys washed up for dinner at the well, and before long they'd formed a noisy but orderly line at the buffet set out in the yard. Mr. Smith spoke a few words of thanks to everyone for helping and added a word of thanks to the Lord for the dinner they were about to enjoy. During dinner, Tim turned to Otto.

"I really like being part of a thrashing crew, and I was surprised at how much water you guys can drink. It makes a guy feel important being on a team which helps us make a living," Tim said. "It makes me feel like a man!"

Otto said, "Feels good, huh? Look! All the guys are heading back to the field. If we don't want to wash all these dirty dishes, we had better get back on the job!"

Tim refilled his water jugs, Otto grabbed his pitchfork, and back to the field they went. Thunder seemed to like his job too, but he remained a little skittish when they rode close to the big thrashing machine. The crew worked through the heat of the day, and well into dusk. Finally, Mr. Smith announced quitting time. They would finish thrashing wheat on the Smith farm tomorrow, and then the next day Tim and his Dad would join the others at the Jackson farm to thrash their oat crop. Toward the end of the day, Tim really felt like one of the team. As he made his way out to the field where his grandfather worked, Tim watched as he reached into his back pocket, took out some chewing tobacco and cut a plug with his pocketknife. Offering him a swig of water, Tim looked his grandfather straight in the eye, like a man.

"Grandpa, since I'm now a part of this thrashing crew, could I have a chaw of that tobacco?' Grandpa Smith thought about it for a few seconds, regarding Tim seriously.

"O.K., I suppose so," he answered, cutting off a plug and handing it to Tim, "Be sure and chew it good, and then swallow. That makes it better!"

As Grandpa Smith went back to work, Tim chewed the wad of tobacco and swallowed. Before long his head began to swim as his stomach lurched dangerously; for some reason he pictured curdled milk, as he got off and gingerly led Thunder back to where his grandpa was working.

"Grandpa, I don't feel so good. I think I'm going to have to go to the house and lie down for awhile. Would you tell Dad he needs to get someone to take my place?"

Grandpa said, "You do look a little green around the gills. You'd better go to the house, and I'll tell your Dad what you said."

Tim vomited more than a few times on his way. Mrs. Smith cast a worried look at her son.

"Tim, you look awful. You better lie down and stay out of the hot sun for a while. Let me get you some water. What happened?"

"I don't know. I asked Grandpa for some chaw and all I did was chew and swallow it like he said, but now I'm really sick to my stomach. I think I'll just lie down a little while and when I get feeling better, I'll get back to work."

Tim fell asleep so fast he never saw his mother shake her head with just the barest smile spreading across her face. She had to hand it to Grandpa Smith! She'd have to remember to thank him for the not so gentle lesson he'd given her son. Tim didn't wake up until the next morning, and right there and then he decided that he'd had his first and his last chew of tobacco. He also decided he needed to have a mind of his own and he didn't have to do something just because he saw others do it – even if it was his own grandpa!

Chapter 14—Cave Adventure

One Friday after Tim finished his chores, Otto came by the Smiths' house.

"I think something weird is going on in that cave along Owens Creek. The other day when I was checking my traps, I saw two men go in this cave and when they came out they were laughing and joking like there was something special in there. I think we should go see what that might be, don't you?"

"I sure do. But what if we are in the cave when they come in? Is there another way out?"

"I don't think so. We'll have to either introduce ourselves to them or stay until they leave and this may take a while, from what I've seen. It's kind of spooky to be running around Amarugia after dark and we both know our parents have told us over and over again to be home before dark. We can tell our folks we might need to stay at the other one's house for the night so we won't be out after dark. Then, if we need to stay in the cave part of the night to see what is going on, our folks won't worry about us." Otto went on to say, "These men usually go in late in the afternoon, so we could get our chores done early tomorrow, and then leave for the cave. Let's walk so no one will see our horses tied outside. The moon should be bright enough for us to walk home, even if it is dark."

"Sounds like a winner to me," Tim said.

As he drifted off to sleep Tim tried to figure out what was attracting these men to that cave. *Did these men find some kind of treasure there? Were they meeting to play poker? Or did they just meet to talk about the crops, hunting and fishing, or what?*

On Saturday, both Tim and Otto woke up when the roosters started crowing. They told their parents they planned to check out one of the caves along Owens Creek. As arranged, Otto told his parents he might stay with Tim overnight. Tim told his folks that there was a good chance he would spend the night with Otto, if they had no objection. In both cases their parents reminded them to be home before dark.

Tim ate a big lunch since he didn't know when he would get to put his feet under the table again, and afterwards he tucked an apple in the bib pocket of his overalls and filled a small bag with some water. Tim was ready to go when Otto arrived, and they walked west toward Owens Creek for the day's adventure.

As they walked along, Tim asked, "Have you heard about the lady who had laryngitis and could not say a word?"

"Nope. Haven't heard that one. What about it?"

"Well, her husband figured out a way they could communicate. He gave her a stick and said, 'Tap one time on the floor for 'Yes' and tap two times for 'No' and 'tap 87 times to tell me to carry out the trash.'"

"Ha, that's funny; my folks will like that one. At least Dad will. We need to remember it just in case we get married some day."

In about 45 minutes they came to the cave where Otto had seen the men come and go. It seemed deserted, so they entered and looked around for any evidence of what the attraction of this cave might be.

"I smell persimmons," noticed Tim. "Do you smell 'em too? Can persimmon trees grow in caves?"

"No. Of course not. I bet that's persimmon whiskey we smell!" realized Otto.

"What's that?"

"Some grownups like to drink it. It's made from layers of persimmon leaves, persimmons, and sugar smashed together, usually in a big crock. After a while it somehow ferments into whiskey if left long enough."

"Where'd you learn that?"

"Some of my friends who come by the Fur Trading Post told me about it, and one of them let me taste a little of it."

The smell became stronger and stronger as they went deeper into the cave. Rounding a bend, they came upon a big pile of persimmon branches.

"There it is." Otto pointed to a glint of pottery through the brush. Sure enough, they found a crock with a hollowed out gourd dipper tucked in beside it.

"I've never tasted any kind of whiskey but sure do like persimmons. Think I could try? Golly, it's dark in here. What is that thing on top of the whiskey? Oh, my gosh— it's a dead frog! Think maybe the whiskey killed him? Maybe I shouldn't try it after all."

"Go ahead," said Otto, "And tell me if you like it."

Tim cautiously dipped his index finger in the liquid on the opposite side of the crock from the frog and put his finger into his mouth. Immediately his mouth puckered up. He jerked his head back and said, "Wow! This tastes like what rotten eggs smell like. A little dab will do me!"

"Just took one sip for me, too," admitted Otto. "Nasty stuff!"

Just then they heard footsteps coming toward the entrance of the cave.

"Quick!" Otto continued. "Put the branches back over the crock and let's go deeper into the cave. We can see and hear them and they won't even know we're here."

The boys watched as two men came into the cave.

"Man, it's hot today. I can't wait to get a taste of that whiskey. It's the best batch we've ever made," said the one with the grey hair and a mustache that looked like it still had some breakfast left in it.

"It's not bad," said the younger man who had a beard. "It took me a little while at first to get used to that persimmon taste. Do you think anyone else knows about this?"

"No, I don't think so. I keep a sharp eye out when I'm making whiskey. Pity the guy who would spy or try to steal this whiskey! Let's lean our guns up against the wall where we can grab them if someone does come snooping. We can blow a hole in them and then bury them at the far end of the cave. If they're ever found, folks will think it's just another murder in Amarugia. Nobody, but nobody, comes between me and my whiskey!"

What they had just heard sent shivers up and down the spines of Tim and Otto. Both of them wished they were safely back home. They felt like trapped animals. All they could do was wait, hope, and pray. In a low whisper, Tim asked, "Do you know either of these guys?"

"No, I don't think so. It's kind of hard to see from this distance, but I'm pretty sure I don't know either of them."

For several hours the men continued their drinking, cursing and complaining about almost everything. Otto and Tim had never heard such foul and vulgar language. Suddenly Tim felt his nose begin to itch and he whispered to Otto, "I think I'm going to sneeze."

"Quick, take your fingers and hold one of your eyes open. Don't let your lids close! A person can't sneeze unless both the eyelids are closed. Whatever you do, hold the eyelids open!

It doesn't matter if it's the right eye or the left one."

Tim quickly took his index finger and thumb and held his right eyelid wide open, and sure enough, it stopped the sneeze.

"Thanks," he whispered, "I never knew that, but it works. If those guys heard one of us sneeze, we would have been dead for sure!"

The two men continued to drink and talk about how they lied to their women about having to go to the store at Everett to get a plug of tobacco. One of them said, "My woman asked me to bring her back some snuff from the store, but I'll just tell her they're all out of snuff. It's probably not good for her anyhow. It 'yellers' the teeth, you know. I like my woman to have pretty teeth even though mine look like you know what."

As the conversation droned on, every once in a while the boys would hear a hiccup, and they knew the men were getting drunk.

After a while the older man stood up and said, "Here's a little deer meat I brought along. Let's use some of those branches to make a campfire to warm it up. We can burn up that frog too. I'm getting tired of him staring at me."

"That's a good idea. It must be way past suppertime. My old lady doesn't like to cook anymore, and I'm not sure she even likes to have me around."

The boys smelled the venison cooking and felt their own stomachs rumble, but all they could do was watch and smell the fragrance.

As the men ate, they discussed what kind of whiskey was best.

"I like this persimmon whiskey better than corn whiskey, and my persimmon trees do me triple duty. I get pelts from the possums I catch eating the persimmons; I enjoy the knockout punch from the persimmons and those leaves; and then I like to eat possum stew. Burp! I'm getting a little sleepy. I think I'll just lie down there on these soft branches and rest my eyes."

The younger guy with the beard said, "It must be getting pretty late. I'm going home." He picked up his rifle and headed for the cave entrance.

"I'm going too, after I rest my eyes with a little nap."

Otto and Tim had enough adventure for one day and were more than ready to get out of that cave.

"As soon as he's asleep," whispered Otto, "We can slip past him and head for home."

Soon they heard the deep loud snoring of the older man. They never realized just how loud the acoustics were in a cave until they heard this drunk snore! They waited about ten more minutes and then started tip-toeing past the sleeping drunk.

As they were about even with him, Otto felt a sneeze coming on, so he immediately reached up to hold one of his eyelids open, but while concentrating on this, he tripped on a rock. The noise woke the sleeping man. He reached for his gun and tried to get up all at the same time. In the process he hit the barrel of the rifle against the crock-pot, which shattered, and the whiskey ran out all over the cave floor. Otto shouted, "Run for your life! Let's get out of here, quick!"

The drunk swung his gun around in the general direction of the running boys and pulled the trigger. Bam! A shot rang out and the bullet went right between them and blasted a chunk out of the side of the cave!

Tim and Otto must have set some kind of record for exiting the cave amid the cursing and shouting of the old guy.

"They got away; they got away; all my whiskey is gone and all I shot was a hole in the side of this blankety blank cave! I must be having a nightmare; how can all this happen to me?"

The boys ran as fast as they could all the way to Otto's house. Otto was still panting when he said, "Whew, were we lucky. We could have been killed tonight! My folks have already gone to bed. It must be close to midnight. Let's sleep in the barn with Lightning so my folks won't know how late we got home. They will think I'm at your house, and your folks will think you are staying overnight with me. If we don't tell them, they won't know what trouble we got into tonight. I'll slip in the house and bring us back something to eat."

"O.K. with me, I'm starving. A straw bed will feel good, and I can eat anything. I'm so hungry I probably could eat a pickled frog sandwich. It just feels good to be alive! No more midnight cave adventures for me. It gives me the creeps just to think about what could have happened to us tonight. I've got the shakes now and it isn't even cold!"

Otto agreed, "We both smell like persimmons. Our parents would probably think we've been drinking persimmon whiskey. I hope Lightning doesn't mind smelling persimmons the rest of the night and I dread to think what Dad and Mom will say in the morning when they find out what happened and what time we got home."

Otto slipped into the kitchen, fixed a couple of sandwiches, grabbed a handful of cookies, and slipped back to the barn. After they ate, the boys were so exhausted they soon fell fast asleep on the hay.

The next morning, as soon as they heard the roosters crowing, the boys got up, and Tim headed for home. When he arrived, both his parents were waiting for him as he tried to sneak in the back door of the kitchen.

"Timothy B. Smith, where have you been all night?" Mr. Smith asked in a stern voice.

Tim tried to look calm when he answered, "Remember, I said if Otto and I were kinda late getting back, I would stay overnight with him?"

"Yes, we remember," Mrs. Smith said.

"But when I called his Mother just after eleven, she said that you and Otto were not at their house. Then, she called back later and said they saw you two slip into their barn around midnight. We were worried sick! How do you explain what happened young man?"

Tim swallowed hard and looked down at the floor and after a second or two, which seemed like an eternity, he said, "I lied and I'm sorry. We got back from the cave late because we ran into some big trouble there. Since we thought you all would think we were sleeping at the other's house, we just slept out in the barn at Otto's place. We didn't think about you all worrying about us. We should have told you what happened as soon as we got home."

"Son, do you think we were just born yesterday? Didn't you know that we would check to be sure you made it back O.K.? We do this because we love you. You know your Mother and I were your age once, and we know that adventures are fun, but they can also be dangerous. Tell us what happened."

Tim then told them all that happened that evening.

"Do you realize you might have been killed? Those men may be criminals who steal and kill as a way of life."

"You're right. Those guys could have killed us." Tim agreed. "And these men could have killed Lightning and Thunder if we'd taken them with us."

"I hope you and Otto have learned a lesson," Mr. Smith continued. "You need to confide in your parents, especially when there may be danger involved. There is usually a good reason why parents don't like for their children to be running around the countryside after dark. You know, some places have an unwritten law that says they shoot strangers after dark. Your Mother and I have talked it over. We have decided you are to be punished for the rest of the month. And remember, none of us can ever fool God. We love you, Son, but we want you to be safe, also. We do appreciate the fact that you admitted you lied and that you are sorry for what you have done. We are thankful you are back safe and sound."

"You're right. I should have told you what happened and not try to cover up our getting back so late by staying in the Swartz barn overnight."

Approximately the same thing occurred at Otto's house the next morning. Otto also was punished for the rest of the month and had to do extra chores. This made him realize that some-times—future Kings need discipline, too. He realized his parents loved him and wanted the communication between him and them to be frank and open, so they could function well as a family. For the rest of the month, chores were never done better, and even extra tasks were undertaken to show they had learned their lesson. And the lure of the cave had definitely lost its appeal.

Chapter 15 — Brush Arbor
Camp Meeting

One afternoon Tim drove his mother to the store in Everett to get some groceries. They noticed several adults and children working in a field near the store. Some of the men were driving long poles into the ground and some of the older boys were weaving other slender poles to make a roof. Then branches filled with leaves were placed where they would make a shade and shed some water in case of a rain. Others hastily fashioned long benches.

"What's going on?" they asked the clerk. She said, "Starting Wednesday morning a brush arbor meeting will begin here. They are building it now."

"What's a brush arbor meeting?" Tim wanted to know. The lady behind the counter explained that preachers—circuit riders—would often send word ahead of their approximate time of arrival in a community. Often the crowds are so large a small church building can't hold them all, so they meet in the brush arbors. Some people travel two or three days to attend and will camp near the brush arbor where there is plenty of room for everyone. The clerk said one of the families in the Everett community had offered one of their 40-acre fields for the meeting.

Tim asked, "May we go, Mom?"

"Let's talk it over with your dad this evening." The Smith and Swartz families felt a need for some spiritual help, especially since Tim and Otto's cave adventure.

That evening the Swartz family joined the Smiths for a promised capon dinner. After supper, while the girls helped their mothers with the dishes, the fathers sat out on the porch. Mr. Swartz was the first to speak, "You know, they're both good boys. You and I might have done the same thing when we were their age."

"You're right, of course, but there are certain things we can do to help them grow up in this crazy world," Mr. Smith said, "I think we've been so busy making a living, we almost missed making a life. I know our family has been leaving the Lord out of our lives."

"I think you've hit the nail right on the head. I hear there's a brush arbor camp meeting coming to Everett in a few days. When I lived in Kentucky, I attended one of those meetings and it changed my life. I even joined the Methodist Church. But since I moved here, opened the Fur Trading Post, got married, and started my family, I've been so busy I've just about left the Lord out my life, too."

"I understand what you're saying. Our Bible just sits on the shelf and gathers dust because we say we're too busy to read it. When we first moved to the farm, we planned on attending church—at one time or another. Mae, Betty, and I are all baptized as Baptists—but on Sundays we usually work on odd jobs. It seems like we never get caught up, and we never will attend church if we wait until we have time. Mae mentioned that Tim wanted to go. I say we make some time to attend some of those meetings."

Mr. Swartz smiled and said, "You know, since the boys have admitted they don't know it all, this may be the best time in the world for our families to make some major spiritual decisions, because we don't know it all either, do we?"

In the meantime, in the kitchen, their wives and daughters were also discussing the meeting. Betty and Dovie were excited to attend and learn some of the gospel songs and hear some of the testimonies.

On the evening of the first meeting, Otto and Tim were among the first ones there. The boys went early so they could catch up on all the news about where the fish were biting and how the fur bearing animals were doing in other parts of Amarugia. Also it was interesting to know how the crops did in the prairie areas. If things were going well, the people would say, "We're living high on the hog this year." Otto always liked talking to the neighbors and finding out how the foals which Lightning had sired, were doing. Tim also liked to visit with 4-H members who were fattening calves to butcher later in the fall. Just to see their school teacher and 4-H leaders at the camp meeting encouraged the young people to realize that spiritual

things were important. Betty invited several other teenagers, and they always found lots of things to talk about, especially boys and their girl friends. Dovie spied Sally there and they always liked to talk about horses, quilting, and making taffy. The adults usually talked with their neighbors about their families and how the crops and livestock were doing, as well as comparing their aches and pains. The social time before the services was very important for the meeting to take on a personality all of its own. Also, some people only talked about spiritual things at meetings like this.

Tim presented Otto with a new idea, "You know, since we have been grounded, I've been looking over my Bible. I checked out the Ten Commandments and now I realize I have broken several of them."

"Which ones?" Otto asked.

"Well, for starters, one says to obey your father and mother. I didn't do this. How many times did they tell me not to stay out after dark because it's too dangerous? I not only disobeyed, but I tried to get them to think I was just spending the night at your house. I've never thought of myself as a sinner. I've never killed anyone or robbed a bank or anything like that, but I've broken the very first commandment which says, 'Thou shall have no other gods before Me.' In other words, I've let my interests and plans take first place in my life instead of asking God what He wants me to do with my time and energy. I hardly ever think of God, much less 'Have no other gods before Him.' I generally put what I want to do first and only think of God when I get into trouble or get sick. Then, there is also that commandment that says, 'You shall not covet or want something that belongs to your neighbor.' That means even a horse or other livestock. Probably at least half of the people in Amarugia covet Lightning—me included. Does that make sense?"

"Yes Tim, it makes sense. I think I have been so busy having a good time and my ambition to become King has not left room for God. My dad suggested that we go and listen to what these fellows have to say. I've been reading my Bible, too. More and more I am becoming convinced I should be living my life according to the Bible, not just doing what I want to do."

As time drew near for the meeting to get underway, many families started arriving in their buggies and wagons. The field was within walking distance for Tim and Otto's families, which meant they did not have to be concerned about taking care of their horses. It also meant that after the afternoon meeting, they could return home, do their chores, and sleep in their own beds each night. The Smith and Swartz families attended the camp meeting faithfully. Otto and Tim made new friends with some of the boys their age. Betty and Dovie found many of their school friends there, as well as several from 4-H.

Even the Indians from the surrounding flat lands came and sat with their tribes. Otto said he heard that as many as 500 Indians had attended some of the camp meetings held near Harrisonville a few years ago. "Which tribes?" Tim asked.

"Many came from the Osage and Delaware tribes. Do you know why the Delaware Indians were called the 'Grandfather' tribe?" Tim shook his head.

"Because other tribes respected them as peacemakers and let them settle their disputes. Some of these tribes even signed the first peace treaty with the newly formed United States Government."

Many southerners moved to the Highlands of Amarugia from the hill country of eastern Kentucky, eastern Tennessee, and western Virginia. Northerners moved to the Prairie from Ohio, Indiana and Illinois. Most of them lived on the prairie flat lands and they enjoyed talking about cattle, horses, and their grain crops, and everybody enjoyed talking about their families. Fur trappers, sawmill workers, renters, and owners of the land also filled the wooden benches beneath the brush arbor. Most of the ladies sat together and most of the young people did likewise.

Each morning, afternoon, and evening, traveling evangelists took turns preaching. Brother David was one of the most popular, leading hymns like *When the Roll Is Called Up Yonder*, *Amazing Grace*, *Bringing In The Sheaves*, and *Shall We Gather At The River?*, to the sounds of a pump organ that had been brought in by wagon. The leaders encouraged interesting testimonies from those who converted to Christianity during the meetings. Even King David, his wife, and some of his court attended some of the meetings. Often the meetings went well into the night during this four-day period.

The revival preachers waxed eloquently from the tall tree stump that served as a pulpit. They were from several different denominations. Each had his own style and method of delivery. After a couple of days of preaching, people began to think more about spiritual things, and often the conversations included questions about the Lord and how to have a proper relationship with Him.

Tim said, "You know, all this talk about sin reminds me why horses are so smart. They know better than to bet on people."

"Yeah, that's right. And did you know that a race horse is the only animal on the face of the earth which can take 20,000 people for a ride, all at the same time?"

"I hadn't thought of that before, but you are right. The devil sure has a lot of different ways to get people addicted to bad habits."

Brother Steven spoke of sinners being in the hands of an angry God. He preached about the way he saw the world, with people trying to walk over the pits of hell on rotten planks. He pounded on his Bible so hard he almost made the stump sway. Tim looked at Otto with wide eyes. Otto returned the stare with eyes equally alarmed.

"If you fall into the pits of hell," he thundered, "You'll fry like a sausage!"

That evening Mr. Smith told his family that when he was a small boy, some well meaning lady in the church he was attending told him if he didn't go to the front of the congregation and tell the minister he wanted to be saved, he would go to hell. He said he felt like he was pushed into going forward, and he dropped out of church because of that.

The boys noticed that different sections of the audience responded to certain preachers differently. The "hill people" responded more to Brother Steven's emotional preaching, while the "plains people" they knew, responded more to Brother David with his calmer presentation. Some of the other evangelists told of the love of God which caused Jesus to give His life on the cross as the payment for our sins. Some in the audience waved their arms and broke out into tears.

Each in his own way presented Jesus Christ as the Lamb of God who takes away the sins of the world when a person confesses his sins and puts his faith in Jesus as his Savior and Lord. They preached that Jesus was crucified and buried, but on the third day, He rose from the grave, proving His power over sin and death. They explained He did this because He loves everyone and wants everyone to go to heaven when he or she dies. Brother David put it best: "Listen as I read from

John, chapter three and verse 16 in the Bible. It says, 'God so loved the world that He gave His only begotten Son, that whosoever believeth in Him should not perish, but have everlasting life'."

When the preacher gave the altar call to come forward to indicate one wished to have this salvation, several adults and children usually went forward. Some people made sounds that sounded like another language and when asked, one man who'd even started barking like a dog responded, "I'm barking at the devil." (He thought he had the devil up a tree.) Those who became more emotional were led to a special area where they got their emotions under control again. An older lady with knotted hands and white hair got so excited she almost fainted, and Doc Brown had to bring over the smelling salts.

One afternoon, Otto poked Tim in the ribs and whispered, "Look over there. Isn't that the man with the beard we saw in the cave? Do you suppose he is here to confess his alcohol and cussin' problems?"

"You know, he needs to bring that old guy who took a shot at us. He really needs the Gospel too. On the other hand, if he comes and recognizes us, he might take another shot at us!" The next day they looked, but they didn't see either man.

Every day, Otto began to feel more and more that he needed to make a public confession of his sins and declare his faith. Throughout the meeting, he'd begun to feel that God might have better plans for his life than just to become King of Amarugia. Tim also realized that there was a higher power and purpose in this world than just daily pleasures and adventures.

"You know what, Tim? I think I need to trust Jesus Christ as my personal Savior and Lord. Did you hear Brother David yesterday when he read that Jesus said, 'Everyone who shall confess Me before men, I will also confess him before My Father who is in heaven, but whoever shall deny Me before men, I will also deny him before My Father who is in heaven'?"

"The Bible also says, 'We must be born again.' Jesus told a man named Nicodemus that unless a person is 'born again' he cannot even see the Kingdom of God."

"I need to make a decision for the Lord, too," Tim replied. "Why don't we talk with our parents tonight and see what they think about our accepting Christ as our personal Savior."

Later that night, their parents agreed this would be a good time for them to make their decision public. Surprisingly, Mr. Smith even quoted from the Bible.

"Tim, I'm proud to see you make this important decision on your own. You know, Jesus says in the Bible that if we will confess Him before others, then He will confess us before His Father in heaven, but if we deny Him before others, then He will deny us before His Father."

"Thanks for your support, Dad. I had no idea you knew the Bible so well."

The Smith and Swartz parents became aware that their boys were growing up and only the Lord could be with their families at all times, in all places, and in all kinds of situations.

The next day when the altar call was given, Otto and Tim told Brother David they were sorry for their sins and they wanted to trust Jesus as their personal Savior. "Amens" and "Hallelujahs" filled the arbor when they responded to the altar call. Both boys said they wanted to be baptized as well.

That afternoon there was great rejoicing in the Smith and Swartz homes.

Mrs. Swartz, though pleased for Otto, still held to the old Indian ways of worshipping the creation rather than the creator. She wanted to see if all this made a difference in Otto and Tim before she made a public decision to accept the Lord Jesus Christ as her Savior. Dovie had also decided to wait, wanting to see what her mother chose to do.

On the last day of the meeting, all four evangelists, the converts, and their families gathered on the bank of the nearby Millers' pond, and Otto and Tim joined them. One by one, the preachers brought their new flock of converts down into the edge of the water. The Methodist pastor let his new members decide whether to be sprinkled or immersed. Otto chose immersion, and when he reached the water, the pastor put his left hand behind Otto head and raised his right hand in the air, "Inasmuch as you have trusted in Jesus Christ as your Lord and Savior, and in obedience to His command, I baptize you now, my brother, in the name of the Father, the Son, and the Holy Spirit." At which time, he brought his right hand with a handkerchief over Otto's nose as he leaned him back completely under the water. As soon as he was completely immersed, he immediately raised him up to a standing position. Otto made his way to the nearby bank of the pond and the Baptist pastor motioned for Tim to come and be baptized. Still dripping, Tim joined Otto and together they walked to a nearby shelter where they changed into dry clothes. They congratulated each other and hurried to greet their smiling families and their new spiritual brothers and sisters in Christ.

FALL—1910

Chapter 16—Chicken Thief

One morning, Betty came into breakfast with a puzzled look on her face. "Something bothering you, Betty-Boo?" asked her father.

"Have you sold some capons and not mentioned it?" she asked.

"No. Of course not. Why do you ask?"

"You know I count them every day when I feed them. We should have 20 capons. We did yesterday! But, when I counted them today, there were only 15."

Mrs. Smith set the iron skillet to the side and turned to the conversation. "Honey, you don't suppose a weasel or fox it getting into our chicken house?" she asked, alarm sneaking into her voice.

"Did you see any tracks around or any hole where some animal could get in?" Chimed in Tim.

"I did see a few footprints which looked like they were made by a man."

Neither Mr. Smith nor Tim said they had been around the hen house since the rain earlier in the week.

"Otto once told me that thieves often toss meat to dogs to keep them quiet," offered Tim.

"That may be what happened with our capons," Mr. Smith said thoughtfully. "Someone may be stealing them to eat or maybe to sell. We'll need a plan to catch him. He may come back tonight since there isn't any moonlight whereby he could be seen. Surely the dogs will start barking before he has a chance to throw them something to eat. We'll wait with our flashlights and guns, and then give him enough time to get into the hen house and catch him in the act. With any luck, we'll haul him straight to King David's court in the morning."

Tim asked, "Is it O.K. if I invite Otto to help us and then spend the night? He and I could help turn our flashlights on the thief and tie his hands behind his back." Mr. Smith turned to his wife and asked, "Mae, O.K. with you? Otto does tie real good knots and we can always use another hand if we catch someone. Almost hate to say it, but it doesn't hurt that he's a good shot, too."

"Sure."

Otto arrived eager to go on watch, especially since his father loaned him the revolver. After Otto arrived, they talked about why there was so much stealing in Amarugia. Mr. Smith said, "One reason is because there are so many poor people here. If the crops are not good, many cannot raise the food they need for their families. Also, some are lazy and some others are greedy. Some people don't think about God seeing them as they steal. I guess they believe God can't see in the dark! Then too, some just enjoy the excitement of stealing."

Mr. Smith told the boys to wait there and he would take another look around the chicken house. Tim turned to Otto and said, "These flashlights remind me of a joke I heard. Want to hear it?"

"Sure. What is it?"

"Well, this family was visiting the Everglades in Florida. The teen age son asked the tour guide a question. He asked, 'Is it true that crocodiles and alligators won't attack you if you are carrying a flashlight?'

"The guide answered, 'It all depends on how fast you are carrying that flashlight!'"

The joke eased the tension, and Mr. Smith suggested the boys stay in the house and get some shut-eye. Before long, only the occasional moo of a cow or random hoot of a hoot owl stirred the dark, still night.

Mrs. Smith and Betty were to stay inside by the phone so they could call Mr. Swartz if they needed more help. They also had a shotgun for their protection.

Tim, near the end of his watch, had just started to nod off to sleep when Jack and Pumpkin began to bark. He didn't even have to wake his dad and Otto, who'd instinctively grabbed for their guns and flashlights. As suddenly as they'd started, the dogs quit barking.

"Someone must have thrown them some meat," Otto whispered.

In a low voice, Mr. Smith gave the boys a few last-minute instructions.

"Let's wait a few minutes to give whoever it is time to get into the hen house. I'll do the talking. You boys hang back in the shadows, so the thief won't recognize you."

After what seemed like days, the three crept quietly to the door of the chicken house. They peered into the open door and they saw a shadowy figure slowly walking up to the chicken roost where the chickens were resting. They could see all this by the flashlight he had placed on the ground. His rifle was leaning against the wall. They watched as he picked up his flashlight and focused the light in the eyes of a capon, lifted it off the roost, tied its legs together, and put it in a gunnysack. He put three more into the same sack. Just as he reached for another one of the fat capons, Mr. Smith stepped into the open doorway, turned on his flashlight, aimed his rifle at the man and in a loud voice shouted, "Drop that sack and put up your hands! Don't even think of reaching for your gun or you're a dead man!"

The sound of Mr. Smith cocking his rifle ricocheted off every single board of the chicken house.

The man released his hold on the sack, raised his shaking hands, all the time whimpering, "Don't shoot! Don't shoot! I'll do anything you say. Just don't kill me!"

When Tim turned his flashlight on the man and Otto grabbed the intruder's rifle to unload it, the boys could barely contain their surprise. The chicken thief was none other than the drunk who'd shot at them in the cave! Even now they could smell persimmon whiskey.

"Keep your hands up and you won't get hurt," ordered Mr. Smith.

"What's your name?"

"They call me Sloan," he said.

"Search Mr. Sloan and tie his hands behind his back." Otto and Tim did as Mr. Smith asked. They stayed behind him so he wouldn't recognize them.

"We don't take kindly to chicken thieves around here. Why were you stealing our capons?"

"I didn't think you'd miss a few. You have so many."

"So this isn't the first time! Those were your tracks we found yesterday!"

Sloan remained shamefully silent. Mr. Smith led him back to the barn where he put him into one of the empty corn cribs. He left his hands tied behind him.

"You may as well try to get yourself some shut eye. We'll be watching!"

Satisfied the heavy cord would keep the culprit secure for the remaining few hours before dawn; Mr. Smith locked the crib door with a chain and padlock and met the boys back in the yard.

Tim could barely contain his excitement, "Dad! That's the old guy who took a shot at us in the cave!"

Mr. Smith raised his eyebrows.

"I think he was so drunk that night he probably wouldn't recognize us, but I'm glad he didn't get a look at us, but we can't be sure," added Otto.

"You're absolutely right, Otto. I think it best you boys not let him see you tomorrow. We'll need to call your dad once the sun comes up, and ask him to go with me to King David's court. Otto, if you'd help Tim with the morning chores, I'd appreciate it. I'm going to sit just inside the barn door in case he tries to escape. The capons will be O.K. in the sack on the back porch. We'll take them along as evidence when we go to the court. Boys, if you think you can hold down the fort for the day, I'll ask your mother, Tim, to go with us as another witness."

Mr. Smith continued, "When you've finished up the chores here, I want you to head on over to the Fur Trading Post until we get back from court."

"Thanks, Mr. Smith. I'm sure my folks will appreciate that."

"No, thank you, Otto. We couldn't have caught this scoundrel without your help. Now why don't you boys try to get a little sleep? You've got a long day ahead of you tomorrow."

"If it's all the same to you, Mr. Smith, why don't I head back to our place, catch my Dad up, and we'll meet you back here at sunup? That way we won't wake up everyone on the party line, and you'll have plenty of time to get to court and get on the docket early."

"That sounds like a fine plan, Otto. Heck of a good head on those shoulders, Son. Tim, you can learn a lot from your friend here!" Tim smiled; he'd figured that out a long time ago.

"And let's remember to ask the Lord to guide us at the court to do and say the right things."

When the roosters began to crow, Mrs. Smith and Betty had breakfast ready and on the table. Mr. Smith had taken some food and given it to Sloan. Mr. Swartz arrived in his four-seat buggy around sunrise. He and Mr. Smith took Sloan out of the barn and they loaded him into the buggy. Mr. and Mrs. Smith sat in the front seat while Mr. Swartz and Sloan sat in the back. They'd tied Sloan's hands together and Mr. Swartz held the end of the rope.

As the boys dug into their chores, they wondered what would happen to Sloan and if this would be the last they would see of him.

Tim, Betty, and Otto finished up the chores and then went to the Trading Post to help Mrs. Swartz and Dovie take care of business. When the others finally returned, Mrs. Swartz insisted they come to their house for a bite to eat. On the way, Betty embarrassed the boys by pointing out how brave they'd been. Dovie took it all in and asked several questions. They all anticipated the prayer that Mr. Swartz asked Mr. Smith to lead before their meal. He thanked the Lord for keeping them safe and asked that Sloan might see the errors of his ways. As the days went by, it seemed the Lord played a larger part in their lives. Now, they were beginning to live, and not just working to make a living. Mr. Smith told them, "He was sentenced to pay us back with two sacks of corn and pay a court fee of one sack of wheat. He was told if he was found guilty of a crime one more time, they would consider using the Bastinado punishment of beating his feet thirty times with canes, three times a day for a month. That threat really scared Sloan and he promised never to steal again. We were asked to leave one of the capons as payment for our court fee and the other three we brought back home. King David ordered two of his men to take Sloan to his house to collect the court fee Sloan owed them and to see he paid us. We followed them to his house and Sloan gave us the two sacks of corn."

"Do you think he meant it when he promised to never steal again?" Tim asked.

Mr. Swartz answered, "He may have meant it at the time, but when he gets under the influence of alcohol, who knows what he'll do. Some of the people I talked to seemed to think Sloan used to be a bushwhacker."

"What's that?" Betty asked.

Otto piped up, "That is the name given to a person who killed Confederate or Union sympathizers. Some of them settled in this part of Missouri. This part of the country was so evenly divided in their loyalties that some people, even in the early 1900s, hesitate to trust each other."

After supper, Mr. Swartz drove the Smiths back to their house.

"Karl, I really appreciate all the help today. And please thank Spring Bunny again for such a wonderful dinner. Next time, we'll have capon here."

"Happy to help B.J. That's what friends are for. Have a good night."

"You too, Karl."

Chapter 17—Watermelon Caper

Knowing that most of the fruits and vegetables had been canned or dried, Betty asked her parents if she could spend Saturday night at her friend Mary's house.

"Sounds fine with me. Betty, you've worked hard this summer and deserve a little time off with your girlfriend. Be sure you are in their house before dark."

"Don't worry, Daddy, I'll be careful. Tim can take me there and then you'll know I arrived safely."

Mary and her friend Joan were waiting when Betty and Tim arrived.

"I would like for you all to meet my friend Joan. Joan, these are my friends, Betty and her brother Tim. Joan is my cousin from Kansas City and she is spending a few days with us."

"It's nice to meet you two. I've been looking forward to visiting out here in the country. I've lived in the city all my life."

"Come on in, Betty, and bring your things. I'll show you where we'll sleep tonight. It's good to see you, Tim. Guess I'll be seeing you at school next week."

"Guess you will. Goodnight, Betty. Mary. Nice meeting you, Joan," he answered as he turned the buggy around and headed for home.

Mary showed Betty the single bed where she would sleep, where the water bucket was located, and how to get to the outhouse. She and Joan would sleep in the double bed.

"My folks have gone to the grocery store in Everett to pick up some things for supper and will be back pretty soon. I have planned something very exciting for us to do this evening right after supper."

"What's that?" Betty and Joan wanted to know.

"I know where there is a melon patch about three-quarters of a mile from here. I've heard farmers say they plant a few extra seeds because young boys often come at night and steal some of them when they get ripe. The melons are getting ripe now and this evening would be a good time for us to get a watermelon. What do you think? Won't that be exciting? Whoever said, 'Life on the farm is dull'?"

"Oh, I don't know about that," said Betty. "My folks want me to be in the house before dark."

"It'll be O.K. It won't be really dark yet. It'll only be twilight. We want it to be light enough we can see the melons and yet not light enough that the farmer can recognize who we are. We all have on blue jeans and I have three of my dad's caps we can wear. We'll look just like boys from a distance."

"Oh yes, let's do it," Joan interjected. "Then I'll have something exciting to tell all my friends in Kansas City."

"Well, I guess so," Betty haltingly said, "If you're sure we'll be back before it gets real dark."

"No sweat. We'll be back in plenty of time to get a good night's sleep and we'll have a big feast of watermelon tomorrow."

By this time Mary's parents had returned, and supper was soon prepared and on the table. Mary told her parents she was going to take the girls for a little ride before it got dark. She said she and Betty wanted to show Joan the school and a few of the other sights around Amarugia. After supper, the girls cleared the table, and washed and dried the dishes in record time. Just as the sun was setting, three girls got into Mary's buggy and headed down the road toward the schoolhouse. By the time they passed it, the shadows began to fall and Mary handed out her dad's caps to Betty and Joan. She also gave each one of them one of her dad's old pocket knives to cut the melon from the stem. She then drove them to the melon patch. When they arrived, a pale half-moon was in the east giving them just enough light to see the melons. Mary stopped her pony along the middle of the patch and tied him to one of the fence posts.

"Hurry," Mary said, "We don't want to stay here any longer than we have to. Let's climb over this woven-wire fence and pick out the ripest melon we can find and bring it back to the buggy. Climb near the post because it is stronger there, and also you can hold onto the post as you climb."

In just a few minutes all three girls were in the patch and were going from melon to melon, thumping them with their fingers to see if they were ripe. Soon they had three melons. Mary climbed over the fence first and they handed the melons to her and she laid them on the ground by the fence. Then the other two girls climbed over the fence. They loaded the three melons in the back of the buggy, untied the pony, and were ready to leave just as a loud voice rang out.

"Who's there? What are you all doing in our melon patch?"

Then, POW! POW! Gunshot pellets tore through the leaves in the tree top just above their heads. The girls screamed; the pony reared up on his hind legs as Mary cried out, "Let's get out of here before we all get killed!" The pony seemed to understand English too, as he raced toward Mary's house. Too scared to talk, they arrived in just a few minutes. She pulled up behind their barn.

"I don't think they followed us," she said. "Hurry; let's hide these melons in the straw here in the barn. I'll not tell my folks yet what happened tonight. They'll just get upset and then nobody will be happy."

The three girls went directly to their bedroom when they came into the house. Mary yelled down to her mother, "Mom, we're home. We're kind of tired so we're going to bed early. Good night! Love you all!"

Mary's parents were a little puzzled at the girls' sudden fatigue but later when they heard them giggling, they relaxed. Her mom even had to call out twice, "Girls, it's time to settle down."

The next morning, as soon as the first rays of sunlight trickled through the window, the girls slipped out of the house, eager to taste a plug out of each of their melons. When they got to the barn and uncovered the melons, they had a big surprise.

"These things aren't watermelons!" Betty exclaimed. "These are green pumpkins! We can't eat these things!"

Sure enough, they had stolen green pumpkins instead of ripe watermelons. At first they laughed at the dumb mistake they had made. Then the reality of what they had done and the danger they had been in, began to sink in and more serious emotions began to show. At first, each girl took a vow not to tell anyone about their foolish mistake except the Lord. Betty pointed out, "We might as well confess what we've done to the Lord because He knows all about it anyway."

They had lots to pray about: thanks that they weren't shot and killed; pleas of forgiveness for breaking the commandment, "Thou shalt not steal"; and in Betty's case, an added plea for forgiveness for not obeying her mother and father about staying out after dark.

Later on Mary did tell her parents what had happened and as time passed, she did a better job of talking things over with them, especially when she had a girl friend visit her or when she stayed overnight at someone's house. Betty shared what had happened with Otto as well as with her parents. Otto said it just proves that no one is perfect and that he was proud of her for admitting that she, too, made mistakes.

Chapter 18—Snipe Hunt

"I think it's just about the right time of the year for us to take Betty and Dovie on a snipe hunt. I don't think either one of them knows what to expect." Tim looked at Otto, with a mischievous grin starting to spread across his face.

"That's a great idea. It'll be fun to teach them not to believe everything they hear even if it comes from someone they love and admire—like us, for example."

Tim continued, "This Friday night would be perfect. The moon will be about half full, just enough light for the snipes to find their way into the open sack the girls will be holding, but not enough light to show that there isn't a single snipe running down the hedgerow. I'll put Jack and Pumpkin on their leashes and leave them at the house so they won't give it all away by showing their disinterest in all those juicy snipes."

"I can't wait," said Otto, "We need to get the ball rolling on this. I'll talk to Dovie and you talk to Betty, and both of us need to talk to our parents so they won't let the cat out of the bag. O.K.?"

"Cat out of the bag; that's funny! Sounds good to me. How about starting the hunt around eight o'clock this Friday evening? I have a couple of gunnysacks the girls can use. Probably about fifty snipes are all they'll be able to get in each bag before we are finished. Right?"

"Yeah. I don't think they would fall for more than two bags. We don't want to make it seem like too big a deal. It has to be believable, you know. I'll copy some information out of my bird book about snipes and draw a sketch of one to show them what they look like. We can tell the girls we'll dress the snipes and then they can cook 'em—anyway they like—fried, baked, boiled, roasted, or any other way."

For the next several days, the two boys did a top-notch sell-ing-job on Dovie and Betty, but they didn't count on Betty being one step ahead of them. She'd heard about the age-old tradition from older girls at school but she played along and acted like she was really excited about going. She didn't tell Dovie or her par-ents she already knew about snipe hunts, so this made the whole thing exciting for her also.

Friday night finally arrived. The cows and the Angus bull had been put into an adjoining pasture so they would not be spooked by the snipes or vice versa. There was no point in getting Captain Midnight involved in a snipe hunt! Dovie could barely contain her excitement. The weather was good and the moon was as de-pendable as a moon can be. Its reflection made the night a bit eerie. Otto and Dovie drove down to the Smith farm in their buggy so they could carry back their sack full of snipes. Tim tied the two dogs by their leashes to their dog houses, and promptly at eight the four of them made their way to the back of the eighty-acre farm.

The boys took Betty and Dovie to where the hedge trimmings formed a straight line, parallel with the living hedgerow itself.

Otto said, "You all stay right here and hold the sack open with one side of the sack touching the ground so the snipes will run into the sack when we scare them this way. They always run in a straight line and will follow the hedgerow and run right into the sack. When you get a sack full—which will probably be about fifty—tie that sack and hold the other one until you get about fifty in it? Then, yell at us to stop beating the bushes and we'll come and help you carry the snipes back to the house. Is that O.K. with you?"

"Oh yes," Betty said "That'll be great. I can't wait until we catch all those snipes!"

If it had been a little earlier in the evening the boys could have seen a big unbelieving smile on Betty's face, but she was a good actress and they suspected nothing. Tim and Otto ran to the other end of the row of dead hedge-brush trimmings and each picked up a stick and began beating on the brush trimmings as they yelled, "Get out of there, you lazy snipes! We're going to beat you to death if you don't get moving! – scat, switch, switch!—you had better get moving or you will get stomped on! There they go! Do you see them, Otto? There they go straight toward the sack. Here they come, girls! Look out! Be ready! There're on their way! They should be there before long!"

Otto shouted, "I see 'em; there're nice and fat, too! Let's slow down a bit so the sack won't run over!"

The moonlight was dim and the hedge row was fairly long, so the girls couldn't see what the boys were doing, but in the cool night air they could hear every word the boys were saying and they could hear them beating the hedge-brush trimmings. After about fifteen minutes, Dovie turned to Betty and asked, "When are all those snipes going to get here? I haven't seen even one snipe go in that sack yet. Am I holding my side of it O.K.?"

Betty said, "You're doing fine, Dovie; we'll just have to practice patience to see how all this turns out. Would you be terribly disappointed if no snipes ran into your sack?"

"Yes, I sure would, and I would be mad, too! Wouldn't you be mad if no snipes ran into your sack after all this waiting for the delicious snipe meat they've been talking about all week?"

"I've never tasted a snipe, Dovie, and I'm not sure I'd like it. Do you think those boys might be playing a trick on us? I don't hear them yelling and beating the hedge brush row anymore. As a matter of fact, I don't hear them at all. I'm beginning to think they may have gone back to the house. It's getting pretty late. I think they must have played a trick on us. Let's wait about fifteen more minutes and if no snipes come, then let's go back to the house."

"O.K. with me. What other choice do we have? You know what? When I make my next pattern for a square in my quilt, I am going to make a picture of a snipe and every time I look at it that will remind me to not believe everything I'm told."

"That's a good idea, Dovie. And just think, we won't have to cook all those snipes after all. That would have been a lot of hard work and who knows how they would have tasted?"

When the girls got back to the house, sure enough, there were the boys with big smiles on their faces right there at the door.

"Where have you been? We have been waiting for you. We decided all that noise in the hedge brush pile must have been rabbits instead of snipes so we just came back to the house."

Dovie tossed the empty sacks on the floor, put her hands on her hips and said, "The next time we go snipe hunting, I want you two boys to hold the sacks. We'll beat the bushes. Turnabout is fair play, yes?" The snipe hunt was seldom mentioned after that.

There was a real live bird on the farm which Tim liked very much. He had a pet crow that summer and fall. The crow liked to eat mulberries in the tree located near their tool shed. Tim would call to the crow and he would answer back. He put water in a tin can and shelled corn on a little platform on top of one of the poles which held the clothesline. At first the mulberries were green in color; then they turned red and finally black when they were completely ripe. They tasted like a blackberry, only not quite as sweet. The crow would stay in the tree and eat mulberries and when the clothing on the clothesline had been brought into the house, he would fly down to the platform at the end of the clothesline where he would eat the corn and get a drink of water. Tim kept telling the rest of the family that he was trying to get the crow to sit on his finger but he would always fly back into the tree when Tim got within five or six feet of him. Then one evening there was a rain and wind storm and after that, Tim never could find his pet crow. Mr. Smith said, "He probably blew away in the storm and either couldn't find his way back or perhaps he found another mulberry tree or something better."

Chapter 19 — The Accident

The town of Drexel, Missouri, was known as one of the mule capitals of the world. Drexel was only about five miles southwest of the Smiths' home; it is located right on the Kansas border. Mules worked in the cotton fields in the South and were used as dependable workers in fields and construction work. Grandpa Smith had owned horses and cows for several years. This was one of the ways Tim's family made their living on the farm. Mr. Smith had the mares bred to the neighbor's jack and when the mules were born and old enough, he trained them to work in a harness and then sold them for a profit. The Smiths had six mares in all.

One day, Mr. Smith brought a big heavy log up between the house and the barn. There he planned to train the mules to work in their harness. He had a heavy chain wrapped around the log to which he would hook up the mule.

After he hitched the mule to the log, he drove the mule around the area pulling the log until the mule became used to the harness and learned to obey the commands. When he pulled on the rein to go right, it put pressure on the bit in the bridle on the right side and he would call out "Gee." For the left turn he would pull on the left rein and call out "Haw" until the mule learned to turn left at these commands. Of course "Get up" and "Whoa" were associated with either a slack rein or a tight rein depending on whether the mule was to start or to stop.

Tim wanted to help break the mules but Mr. Smith said it would be better if he waited a year or two because it was a dangerous job, but he did let Tim hold the mule's bridle while he hooked the unbroken mule to the log. After the mule was hooked to the log, Mr. Smith had Tim sit on the front-porch step and watch him hold onto the long reins as the mule pulled the log around in circles.

Mr. Smith had just put the harness on a foxy, high-strung young mule he decided to break. He had Tim hold her by the bridle as he began to hitch her to one of the heavy logs. Tim watched his father go behind the mule, bend over, and hook the left trace of the harness. When he went to do the right side, he accidently touched the mule's leg. Startled, she kicked her right leg, hitting Mr. Smith squarely in the middle of the forehead with her hoof.

"Hellllllllp!" he called, as he fell backwards to the ground, blood spurting from his head.

Tim quickly turned loose of the mule and ran over to his dad and cried out, "Dad! Dad! What should I do? Talk to me!!" Mr. Smith, knocked unconscious, couldn't answer. He'd shut his eyes, and blood continued to pour from his head. Tim yelled as loudly as he could, "Mom, Betty! Come quick! Dad, talk to me!!"

Tim heard the screen door slam and his mother scream as she seemed to fly from the porch to his side. She dropped to her knees next to her husband and bellowed to Betty, "Quick, call the doctor. Then bring me as many damp dishrags as you can!" She turned to Tim, calmer, "Honey, can you unhook that mule? We need to get her back in the barn." Tim quickly did as his mother asked.

Betty took up the receiver to the party line they shared with fifteen other families. She didn't have time to find out who was already talking on the line, but broke in hurriedly.

"Excuse me, this is Betty Smith and this is an emergency! I need to call the doctor! My daddy has just been kicked in the head by a mule and I'm afraid he might die! Would you please hang up so the doctor can hear me? Thank you. Thank you so much!" Amid the gasps of surprise and immediate offers of prayers, the ladies complied and soon Betty had Dr. Brown on the line.

He told her to keep pressure on the wound and he would come immediately. Satisfied, Betty stuffed a handful of rags into the bucket of water near the sink and ran out the door towards her mother.

Meanwhile, Mrs. Smith had removed her apron and pressed it against the wound as she learned over her husband and checked his pulse. Betty arrived, breathless, with the rags. The coolness seemed to revive Mr. Smith, ever so slightly.

"B.J., Honey, can you hear me?" She cooed. "Say something, please!"

Mr. Smith moaned and mumbled something, but his speech was slurred. She held the cloth in place and told Tim to bring a pillow and get something to shade his dad's head.

Dr. Brown's buggy soon rounded the driveway and before it even came to a complete halt, he'd grabbed his medical bag and rushed to Mr. Smith. Tim tied Dr. Brown's horse to a nearby fence post.

Mrs. Swartz heard Betty's call over the phone. She couldn't leave the Trading Post but sent Otto over immediately. She then got back on the line, to organize some help. On his way to the Smiths, Otto let the neighbors know that Mr. Smith had been kicked in the head by a mule. They ran from their fields and barns toward the Smith place. Unable to do much until Doc gave the go-ahead to move him, several of the men hastily arranged a makeshift pallet from pieces they found in the barn. As soon as Dr. Brown checked the vital signs, and declared Mr. Smith safe to move, the neighbors gently lifted him onto a pallet and into his bedroom.

Dr. Brown busied himself cleaning and dressing the wound as the Smith family anxiously looked on. Finally a groggy Mr. Smith asked, "Where am I? What happened?"

Dr. Brown told him what had happened and that he was fortunate the mule didn't have on horse shoes because the blow to the head could have killed him. He then turned to the rest of the family.

"As it is, he'll have a dent in his skull for the rest of his life, but hard work and healthful living have made him strong. I believe with the good Lord's help he'll make a full recovery."

Even though the doctor had meant to address only Mrs. Smith and her children, everyone had crowded into the house to hear the news. Collectively they breathed a sigh of relief and Dr. Brown offered a prayer of thanksgiving that Mr. Smith's life had been spared. Dr. Brown told them he would check on the patient daily for a while. He gave Mrs. Smith and Betty instructions on how to care for him and told them to call him immediately if Mr. Smith took a turn for the worse. Some of the neighbors talked with Tim and Otto and they worked out a plan to help with the chores for several days.

Mrs. Smith told Dr. Brown they would be by his office as soon as possible to pay the bill for his services. She sent a pound of butter and a loaf of homemade bread with him to show their appreciation for his prompt response. He said for them not to worry about the bill and to be sure and let him know if they ran into any other problems.

In the following days, all the neighbors pitched in and helped with the chores and Mr. Smith made rapid improvement. Within the week his speech became normal again. No one complained about the extra chores because they were so thankful he lived. Betty and Otto helped Tim with the milking, and Otto shelled the corn to feed the calf they were planning to butcher, and he also slopped the hogs.

Though frightening, the accident brought the neighborhood closer together as they cut stove wood, weeded the garden, and mowed the lawn. Each one of them knew they might need help sometime in the future.

It gave Otto opportunity to learn more farming skills and to get acquainted with more of the neighbors as he sought to learn all he could about Amarugia. Of course, it also gave him a chance to spend more time with Betty—something they both enjoyed. Otto was there every day, and they worked as a team, and the time flew by when they were together.

Within a couple of weeks, Mr. Smith began to do more work around the house and barn. The wound healed nicely and thankfully he avoided infection. Gradually he returned to the fields as well. As the doctor had predicted, the obvious dent in his skull remained. The mule did eventually learn to work and went to a buyer with a farm in western Arkansas.

Chapter 20—Making Taffy

To celebrate Mr. Smith's recovery, Mrs. Smith decided to call the girls in the neighborhood together to make some taffy—Mr. Smith's favorite sweet—as a thank-you for all their help the past few weeks.

Saturday arrived, and Mrs. Swartz drove Dovie over to the Smiths in their one horse buggy, before returning to the Trading Post.

Betty helped Dovie out of the buggy with her pans she'd brought to take some taffy back home.

"You're right on time," Betty said. "Come on in. Your mom and my mom will want to visit for awhile and I can show you my dolls and things while they talk." The women had a brief visit and were soon joined by Mrs. Johnson, one of their neighbors. When Mrs. Swartz left, Mrs. Smith called out, "Girls, you can come into the kitchen now. It's time we got down to some serious business. Put on your aprons and wash your hands and we'll get started. Just listen to this recipe:

> *1 cup of sugar*
> *2/3 cup corn syrup*
> *1 1/2 tablespoons of butter*
> *1/3 cup water*
> *Flavoring, as desired.*

Doesn't that just make your mouth water?"

"What kind of flavoring?" Dovie asked.

Betty named several choices: "butterscotch, chocolate or caramel." Everyone agreed on caramel.

"It says to melt 1 1/2 tablespoons of butter in a sauce pan; add one cup of sugar, 2/3 cup of corn syrup, and 1/3 cup of water; and stir until the sugar is dissolved. I'll help with the stirring, O.K.?"

Betty measured the ingredients and pointed out to Dovie how to read the various readings on the measuring cups and spoons.

"What does it say to do now?"

"It says, 'Bring to the boiling point and boil without stirring until it forms a hard ball when dropped into cold water.' We don't have a cooking thermometer so we will just have to keep dropping some of the taffy into some cold water until it forms a hard ball."

"May I do that?" asked Dovie.

"Sure, you and Betty may take turns and we will see which one gets the hard ball first. Betty, we'd better put some more sticks of wood in the stove so it will get the taffy hot enough."

Soon the mixture came to a boil and Dovie and Betty took turns taking a spoon and every few seconds dropping a little into the glass of cold water.

"Look!" Dovie said. "There's a ball. It's just like magic. Let me read what it says to do next."

"Pour onto a marble slab or agate tray which has been slightly moistened by being wiped over with a piece of damp cheesecloth."

"Let me do that," Mrs. Johnson said, "We have to be careful here not to get burned or spill anything." She poured the mixture out onto a clean marble slab and asked Dovie to read what to do next.

"Fold edges over into the center before they have time to get hard; by doing this, the candy will be kept soft, but in doing it, the candy must be disturbed as little as possible in order to avoid 'sugaring' (if the candy 'sugars' then it cannot be pulled to make taffy)."

Then, Dovie said, "You all fold it over; I'll just watch this part. I'm afraid I'll burn my hands or let it slide off the table."

"Betty, Mrs. Johnson, and I can do this part," Mrs. Smith said. "O.K., Betty, I think it's cool enough now. Let's fold it. You take that side and I'll take this one. We'll fold it several times. What does it say to do next?"

"It says as soon as the candy is cool enough to handle, knead it until it becomes firm. What does "knead" mean?" Mrs. Johnson answered, "It means to press and squeeze with the hands." "O.K., we're doing that; what's next?"

"It says to do this until it becomes firm; add flavoring; and then pull it over a hook until it is white in color." At this point Mrs. Smith added some caramel flavoring.

"It says if you don't have a hook, two strong people can be used to pull the taffy. You all are strong, aren't you?"

Mrs. Smith looked at Mrs. Johnson and Betty and said,

"We'd better be, or else we are in a mess. Come on, pull hard! Dovie will cheer us on." After several pulls the taffy began to turn white in color.

"May I help stretch some of it into rolls," Dovie asked.

"Yes, it's cool enough for you to handle and we are about ready to snip it into bars for pieces."

Dovie then read, "Now stretch the taffy into rolls, snip with oiled scissors into bars or one-inch pieces and wrap in waxed paper. Store in an airtight container in a cool dry place after allowing it to sit for a few days in a place of low humidity."

"They forgot something here," Dovie said, "They forgot to say, 'Be sure and taste it to see if it's good to eat.' I'm ready to do that right now."

"We are too," Betty, Mrs. Johnson, and Mrs. Smith said in unison. They handed Dovie a piece, and each sampled one for themselves.

"I believe this is the best taffy I've ever eaten," Mrs. Smith said.

"Me, too," said Betty, "I love that caramel flavor."

"Me, too," Mrs. Johnson added.

"It's the only taffy I've ever eaten and the best, too," said Dovie. Then they snipped the taffy into one-inch pieces and wrapped each piece in wax paper.

"Oh, my goodness," said Mrs. Smith, "I just about forgot the main reason we made taffy. It is to celebrate B.J.'s recovery from his accident." She went to the porch and called, "B.J., come here; we want to get your opinion on something."

"What's that I smell?" he asked, as he walked toward the kitchen.

"Surprise, surprise!" they shouted.

"We want your opinion on how our taffy tastes. Since the doctor told us you are almost fully recovered, we wanted to do this to help with the celebration! Here, have some, and Otto and Tim can get theirs when they get back from fishing. We'll send some home with Dovie for the Swartz family. After we clean up here, Betty, would you take Dovie home? She's been a big help today."

Mr. Smith helped himself to a couple of the taffy pieces and said, "This is some of the best taffy I have ever eaten and I want you to know how much I appreciate having such a loving and caring family and good neighbors like the Johnson and Swartz families."

WINTER—1910

Chapter 21—First Snow

As the days grew shorter and the nights longer, the Smiths had to depend on their lanterns to give them light so they could see to milk the cows and do the feeding chores. In preparation for the long cold months ahead, neighbors got together, cut down trees and cut them into various sizes. The larger pieces were stacked into large wood piles near the house. These could be cut up into smaller pieces where they could be used as kindling in the cook stoves. The larger pieces were used in the heating stove in the living room. Tim and Otto became very good at using an ax, sledgehammer, and wedge.

Tim could not wait for the day when he would be old enough to purchase some purebred dairy cows and have a modern dairy barn. He had learned the lesson of trying to make a profit by taking a calf which was half-Jersey and half-Angus and expect it to gain weight like it should. He kept records on the cost of the grain and hay he fed his calf. Then, when it was butchered, he recorded the value of the beef. The records showed a five dollar loss. He knew he could have made money if he had a hybrid beef calf instead, because that breed of calf would convert more of the feed into beef. Also his 4-H Club experiences had taught him that if they could afford to purchase some registered dairy cows such as Jerseys or Holsteins and sell to a milk company instead of a cheese company, they could receive more money for their milk. But for now, all they could afford was the mixed-breed herd that was on the farm when they moved there.

One day as Betty and Tim came home from school, they smelled smoke in the air.

121

"I hope it's not somebody's house that's caught on fire," Betty said.

"No, look, it's a field that has been set on fire. Dad said many farmers do this in the late fall and early winter. This fire kills off many of the insects so they won't ruin the crops next year. Dad said we'll burn off a field or two next week. We'll use wet gunnysacks to keep the fire from spreading."

"It seems like I learn something new about farming every week. I guess we never will get it all learned. Well, that makes life interesting."

As the soil rested and the fields went fallow, families had more time to spend with each other. As the kids gathered for 4-H meetings, the adults held their Pioneer Club meetings. Over coffee, sweets, and often, cards, they discussed gardening, crops, and conservation practices.

Occasionally, the young people participated in the Virginia reel at the 4-H gatherings. A group of boys would get in a line on one side of the room and a group of girls would line up facing them on the other side. As the music played, the two lines would advance in time with the music until they came face to face. Then, while keeping time with the music, they would retreat to the rear. On the next time when they came forward, they would do what is called "Doo-see-doo-right" and this time would skip completely around the opposite partner and back to the starting position. The next time the lines advanced to the center they did the "Doo-see-doo-left". On the third time forward they joined hands with their partner and skipped to the right. Betty and Otto particularly looked forward to these nights when they'd be able to hold hands and exercise together.

One evening, as the Smiths and Swartzes made their goodbyes, they stepped outside to the beautiful sight of big white snowflakes drifting down from the clouds above. In a couple of days, more than a foot of snow had covered the fields. It didn't take long before they noticed the differences of snow and ice in the small town and snow and ice on an 80-acre farm. The snow drifted in many places into deep drifts and it changed the look of the landscape. In Archie they had only a few paths to clear with a shovel, but on the farm there were 80 acres and one just shoveled a path where it was necessary.

Mr. Smith wasted no time in pointing out all that had to be done. "Tim, before we can get to our chores, we'll have to start digging. You get started on a path to the barn. Betty-Boo, why don't you start one to the chicken house? In the meantime, I'll get started on one to the hog pen and maybe this afternoon Otto can come by and help us on one to the pond."

By mid-morning, they'd cleared the paths and before they headed out for their chores, Mrs. Smith had them all come in for some cocoa. While Tim and his dad tried to coax milk from the cows, Betty tried to feed the chickens. "They seem to have trouble finding the corn and wheat kernels in the snow," she reported.

"They'll find it when they get hungry enough, Betty," her father reassured her. "This is only the first snow of the year and it's a long time until spring. It looks like the temperature is going to stay below freezing for several weeks now. We'll clear out a little spot so they don't get too hungry. They'll get the hang of it."

"I hope so! I'd hate not to have eggs!"

After lunch, Otto and Dovie rode over on Lightning. Otto, Tim, and Mr. Smith, shovels in hand, headed out to clear a path to the pond. Once there, they cut a hole in the ice so the calves and horses could get a drink. Satisfied with their work, they moved on to the back pasture, clearing a path for the other livestock so they could drink from the tank located below the large pond. "We'll have to get in the habit of pitching hay down from the loft for the horses and cows to eat, boys. Otto, if your dad can spare you at the Post, I'd be willing to pay you to help us out right after each big snow fall this winter."

"I'm sure he can spare me a few hours a day, Mr. Smith. I'd be happy to help!"

Finished with their clearing and feeding, they made their way back to the house and found that Betty and Dovie had also been busy. The yard boasted half a dozen snow people!

"I did all the noses and picked out their hats!" Dovie proudly explained. She'd used a combination of corn cobs, carrots and potatoes to startling effect. The boys immediately set out to construct a snow fort and before long, they'd stockpiled more than enough ammunition. Mr. and Mrs. Smith even jumped into the fray and soon the snow balls flew across the yard.

Eventually, Mrs. Smith called the girls in to help her with supper and after filling everyone with warm stew, she sent the Swartzes back home. That evening, she made sure everyone was properly ready for bed. "Does everyone have a hot water bottle?"

"Mama, my toes are still cold. May I have a hot iron too?"

"I think the stove's still warm enough for me to heat one of the sadirons for you. Go grab some newspaper to wrap it, and leave them on the kitchen table for me. I'll bring it up and tuck it in by your toes as soon as it's ready."

"Thank you! This was the best snow day ever!"

"I think so, too, Betty. Goodnight, Sweetheart."

"Goodnight, Mama."

The next morning, after they'd finished with the milking and slopping, Mr. Smith played a little trick on Tim. While in the back pasture he'd shot and killed a jackrabbit. Not as plentiful as the cottontail rabbits which were all over the farm, the jackrabbit had long ears and was larger than the bunny rabbit cottontails. Tim had never been able to creep up close enough to shoot one so Mr. Smith took the jackrabbit he'd shot and propped him up against a dead stump in the pasture. When he got back to the house, he saw Tim coming out the back porch door.

"I just saw a big jackrabbit hopping around in the back pasture a few minutes ago. Do you want to see if you can shoot him?"

"I sure do. Where did you see him?"

"Come on and I'll show you. You can use one of these .22 long rifle shells so we won't spook him by having to get too close."

Tim dived inside and returned with the rifle.

"He was running toward that stump the last time I saw him. There he is. I see his long ears right by that stump. Do you see him?"

"Yes, I see him."

Tim loaded and cocked the rifle, took careful aim, and pulled the trigger. The bullet hit the jackrabbit and he fell over on his side. Tim ran over to claim his prize.

"Thanks for letting me shoot him."

"That's a dandy," said Mr. Smith.

"Go ahead and gut him and hang him up on the shed wall with our other pelts. Your mother says she has enough rabbit and squirrel meat. He'll stay frozen and tomorrow we will take all the pelts to the trading post and sell them."

"I can't wait to show him to Otto!" Tim crowed.

"And I bet he can't wait to see him," his father agreed.

The small pond by the barn had been frozen over for several days, and Mr. Smith said it was safe to play on it. Tim and Betty learned to ice skate and to pull each other around on their sled. One day when Tim was checking out the ice around the edge of the pond, he discovered something which looked like tiny catfish frozen in the ice. He went to the tool shed; brought back a screwdriver and chipped out some of the ice where he saw them. To his amazement, they were tiny catfish which were caught in the ice when the water froze. Pulling them out, he continued poking through the ice until he hit water. Then, gently, he returned the fish into the water. Soon, unfrozen, the little catfish swam away. Tim showed the frozen fish to everybody he could and told them, "Freezing doesn't kill catfish; it just slows them down to a stop."

Chapter 22—Cemetery Visits

One Saturday the temperature was very comfortable, so Otto called Tim on the phone and asked if he would like to go for a ride around Amarugia. Tim was always agreeable for a ride, so he asked his parents if it was O.K. with them. They had no objection, so in a few minutes Otto was at their front door.

Somehow Betty always managed to be closest to the door when Otto came knocking.

"Hello, Otto, come in. Good to see you."

"Good to see you, too;" he said with a wink and twinkle in his eyes. "How do you like living in Amarugia by now?"

"It's great; I love all the animals; I love school, the churches, and the 4-H club; and we have some fabulous neighbors like you and your family."

"I feel the same way. I guess we couldn't ask for much more. Hello, Mrs. Smith. How are you? Is Tim around?"

"Oh, I'm fine, Otto. Tim just went to the pasture to get Thunder. I hear you boys are going for a ride today."

"Yes, I thought we would check out some of the cemeteries around here. Have you seen the Moudy and Everett cemeteries?"

"Nope, we've been too busy to make it to the cemeteries," Betty said.

At that time, Tim came in. "It didn't take you long to get here. Lightning must be feeling his oats today. Yes?"

"You got that right. He's raring to go and he doesn't care where. Is there any place special you would like to visit today?"

"Not really; I've been interested in every place you've shown me so far. Lead away."

"Let's go take a look at the Moudy Cemetery. It's just southeast of the school house. This cemetery is thought to have been in use about 20 years before the Everett Cemetery." Many of the families here wanted to be buried in the Kingdom of Amarugia. Another interesting fact is that the people here were usually buried in wooden caskets. They made their own wooden caskets; they were wider at the shoulder's end and more narrow at the other end. There are thought to be three cemeteries in Amarugia. The Moudy Cemetery was formerly known as the Herrell Cemetery. The Elias Moudy family gave land for its southern expansion. There are also the Williamson and the Everett Cemeteries."

In a short time, Otto led them down a road into the Moudy Cemetery. They tied their horses to a couple of trees and looked at the grave markers.

"Look at this one. They say this is the oldest existing gravestone. It is for Mary F., wife of E. B. Jurd, born June 1, 1822, Departed this life Apr. 22, 1857, AE. 34 yrs, 10 ms. 21 ds."

"Gosh, that's pretty young, but I guess more people died of disease back then."

Otto then pointed to another gravestone which read, "Mary A., dau. of J. M. & E. A. Morton, died Oct. 4, 1868, aged 15 y. 1 M. 5 D. She was the same age as I am now."

Another grave which caught their eye was that of "William P, son of J. & A. Sims, died Aug. 20, 1861, aged 17 Y. 10 M. 7 D." Otto said, "This grave is probably that of the Sims boy who was harmlessly sitting on a rail fence at the southeast corner of Marvin's present farm when an unseen bushwhacker shot and killed him. His parents, Jesse and Ann, came from Virginia and North Carolina."

"I sure wouldn't want to go back to the good old days. Would you?"

"No, I wouldn't either. It's dangerous enough around here as it is. Say, why don't we stop by my house on the way to the Everett Cemetery and I can show you some of the old copies of the *Cass County Democrat*."

"Sure," said Tim. "There is very interesting history all around us."

As they looked through the pages of the *Cass County Democrat*, dated April 10, 1890, they read the column entitled, *"Amarugia Headlight."* It said, *"News scarce again this week. Plenty of rain and lots of measles."* A statement which caught their attention was that which said,

"King David, the enterprising farmer and stock dealer of Amarugia is improving his residence and its surroundings considerable this spring. We hope he may live long and prosper."

After lunch they rode on to the Everett Cemetery where they found many more tombstones and grave markers.

Otto was the first to speak, "Have you heard that some people have been turned away from this cemetery?"

"No; who?"

"It is said that a man named Alexander Cecil—who everyone called Whit—a former sheriff of Floyd County, Kentucky, moved to this part of the country. Sometime after the Civil War, Whit became angry with a black boy who was living with him and threw a stick of stove wood which hit the boy in the head and killed him. He wanted to bury the boy in the Everett Cemetery but the community would not allow it, so he buried him on his own farm—on a slope of a hill west of a little draw. There was another man by the name of Jeremiah Dorsett who was kicked out of the church because he wanted a black person buried in the Everett Cemetery."

"I've never heard that, but I have heard that the reason fences are put around cemeteries is because so many people are dying to get in. Ha!"

"Funny, Tim. You want to read some of these messages?" Otto said, "Here's one which reads, 'OSBORN/ALBERT OSBORN/BORN DEC. 8, 1818/DIED AUG.20, 1904./ —/ MARY OSBORN/BORN SEP.18,1819./DIED FEB.28, 1894./—/ Thou art gone from a world of care/ The bliss of heaven to share./ (north grave footstone:) MOTHER.'"

They looked at several others and Tim said, "It's getting close to time for me to start my evening chores. I'd better get started toward home."

"Me too, and just think, some day we too will probably have a marker similar to some of these. Maybe we should think about what message we would like to leave this world."

Chapter 23—Christmas

The weeks ticked by before they knew it; Christmas was right around the corner. One Saturday afternoon, instead of the usual Pioneer Club and 4-H meetings, the Smiths, Swartzes and some of their friends went hunting for Christmas trees. The Amarugia Highlands had them sprinkled all over the hills. Armed with axes, and full of Christmas cheer and excitement, they gathered with their sleds and horses at the Swartzes house. Tim brought their big sled also, and Thunder did what he always did best—he followed Lightning.

"The Amarugia Highlands are full of cedar trees," said Mr. Swartz. "When you see one you like, give a yell, and we'll stop and mark it. They are all sizes and free for the taking."

Dovie and Betty rode with Otto, and Sally joined Tim and Mr. Smith. Mrs. Smith stayed behind with Mrs. Swartz to pop corn so they could decorate the tree when it was set up in the corner of the living room. Mr. Smith passed on Mr. Swartz's suggestion, "Why don't we ride around for a while and look at all the evergreens which would make a good Christmas tree and then on our way back, stop and cut the trees of our choice. What do you all think of that idea?" Everyone agreed and they spend a couple of hours sledding over the hills and knolls as they enjoyed the sled ride and choosing their favorite tree. Soon the Amarugia Highlands echoed with the singing of *Silent Night, Jingle Bells, O Little Town of Bethlehem,* and *We Wish You a Merry Christmas*. They stopped for a brief rest, and managed to find time to heave a few snowballs at each other. On the way back they soon had a load of trees and they sledded to each neighbor's house where each tree was unloaded.

The Smith house was next to last. Dovie and Sally were all excited about helping Betty string the popcorn to decorate their tree, and the boys were excited about eating the extra popcorn. While

Mrs. Smith and the girls strung the popcorn, Tim, Otto, and Mr. Smith built a stand around a small bucket to hold the tree upright and water was poured into the bucket to help keep it fresh. There was definitely a Christmas Spirit with the fragrance of the pine tree and the smell of popcorn in the air.

The churches at Everett were also in the spirit of Christmas. For several weeks, both the Methodist and Baptist churches had been practicing the Christmas pageant. At Thanksgiving and Christmas, the churches always joined together for the holiday season. The best singers always were given the solo parts and some of the most humble looking played the parts of Joseph and Mary. While those in the pageant rehearsed, other members went caroling. Piled into their sleighs, they'd stop at each farmhouse early in the evening just after the sun had set.

Before long a few packages appeared under the tree at the Smith home. In many families, the young children were told that Santa Claus would bring their presents on Christmas Eve. Tim didn't see any present for him under the tree even though he was familiar with Santa Claus. He had been busy hunting for his wagon for a couple of weeks. He used it to haul in stove wood from the woodpile but he couldn't find that wagon anywhere. He thought someone must have stolen it, because he thought he had looked everywhere. He even looked through the tool shed and the barn. Then one Sunday afternoon he was poking around in the attic and at the back of the attic he spied a beautiful bright red wagon. He recognized it as his wagon at once. It dawned on him that his dad and mom didn't have money enough for a new present, so they had taken his wagon and given it a couple of coats of bright red paint. Tim didn't say anything to his parents about finding his wagon but he thought, *"This is the best Christmas present I have ever received, because I know my parents really love me because they figured out a way to give me something so I won't have to go without a Christmas present from them this year."*

Otto gave Tim a coonskin cap, and he gave Betty a pair of fur-lined house slippers. Tim gave Sally, Otto, and his parents a booklet of jokes he had put together. Betty made several kinds of candy for each family member. She received a nice dress which her mother made at the sewing club. It worked out for everyone to receive a gift of some kind although there was very little money to buy anything.

When Christmas Eve finally arrived, the Swartz and Smith families attended the joint service at the Baptist church. The services were held jointly so families could visit and make new friends.

A doll usually represented the baby Jesus, but this year there was a real live baby who played the part perfectly. He cried and cooed the proper amount just at the appropriate times. They sang carols and the congregation joined with the choir in singing the final hymn, which was *Oh Holy Night*. Afterwards, they returned to the Swartzes' for eggnog, hot chocolate, and pie.

On Christmas morning, the children were the first to gather around the tree at both the Smith and the Swartz homes. At the Smith home there was a bright red wagon which held the other presents. Mr. Smith remarked, "You know, there are worse things in life than being poor. After all, being poor is more like the first Christmas anyway, and many other things are more important in life than things. The love we have for God and for each other can't be bought for any price. Karl and I did kill and dress a deer a couple of days ago so I'll let that venison be my gift to you this year." Mrs. Smith had embroidered a poem to hang on the wall. She said we need to give Jesus a present on His birthday. She made one for her family and another one for the Swartz family. Before the presents were given out, she read her poem to all.

A Poem

by Christina Rossetti

What can I give Him, poor as I am?
If I were a shepherd, I'd give Him a lamb.
If I were a wise man, I'd do my part.
But what can I give Him?
I can give Him my heart.

SPRING—1911

Chapter 24—Planting Time

Eventually the cold days and nights began to give way to sun-kissed mornings and milder evenings. The birds began to sing, the jonquils started blooming, and even Jack and Pumpkin got caught up in the excitement of a new season. All the farmers knew they needed to be making plans for getting the seeds into the soil for the new crops. The Smiths and their friends in the Pioneer Club and the children in the 4-H Clubs had been sharing information and plans with each other for weeks. The Smiths were especially looking forward to their first planting. Last year all they had to do was cultivate and harvest the crops.

One evening, Mr. Smith called the family around the kitchen table. "Let's put our plans down on paper so we can picture what we need to do to have a successful year. First we need to make some cold frames and get some things growing."

"What's a cold frame?" Betty wanted to know.

"A cold frame is an enclosure for growing plants. They vary in size but the front boards are usually about 12 inches high. Two sideboards slant upward from the front to the back. A sloped glass cover allows the sunlight to enter and permits water to run off the top of the box. We'll mix some chicken or horse manure with some soil for rapid growth. If we plant seeds and plants now, they'll be ready to put in the ground in 4 to 10 weeks."

"Are there any plants we can put in the ground before the danger of freezing is over?" Tim wanted to know.

"Yes, we can start with our potatoes, lettuce, cabbage, spinach, broccoli, onions, and radishes. A little frost won't bother them."

Mr. Smith continued, "What do you all think about having a truck patch in addition to our garden? That way we can have a big strawberry patch and room for all kinds of melons, cantaloupe, and squash. We can make strawberry preserves and can the extra pumpkin and squash, as well as the sweet corn and berries. We can put our truck patch just south of our little pond and then we can irrigate when we run into a dry spell, and believe me, they say that will happen sooner or later."

By bedtime the notes and sketches filled several pages.

"This has really been fun this evening," said Mrs. Smith. "I think the Lord has given us all a desire to be creative. Why don't each of us in our prayers tonight thank the Lord for the many opportunities He has given us on the farm, and ask Him to help each of us to do our best to help these plants and animals grow and bear much fruit?" They all agreed as they filed off to bed.

Mr. Smith kept busy plowing, disking, harrowing, and generally preparing the soil. Mr. Smith first hitched up two of the mares to a plow and plowed up the garden and truck patch areas. Then he ran the disk and harrow over those areas before the entire family took part in cutting the potatoes into pieces, being careful to leave at least one eye in each piece. They set out the plants from the cold frames and planted all kinds of seeds. Otto and Dovie helped their family put in a garden also, although Mr. and Mrs. Swartz had only one milk cow and a few ponies, because the trading post kept them busy most of the time.

Spring cleaning took on a whole new meaning when it came time to clean out the barn and chicken house. They loaded the manure into the spreader, and pulled it across the fields and pastures to fertilize the ground. Mr. Smith was easy on Tim when it came time to clean out the outhouse. Mr. Smith said he would clean it out himself, because he remembered his dad didn't make him help with this job either. He did ask Tim to keep the bucket in the outhouse full of corn cobs.

The Smiths also procured two hives of bees. "To fertilize the plants, and then we get to share some of their honey," Mr. Smith pointed out. They kept a container with some sugar water near the hives. When the time was right, Mr. Smith fired up the smoker, then squeezed the handle, releasing a puff of smoke. He put on his protective net over his head and wore a long-sleeved shirt. After a few puffs of smoke into the hive, Mr. Smith would lift off the lid and scrape off the honey into a big container. He seldom got stung, but when he did, he said it was worth it.

It seemed like spring came all at once. The April showers came and the ground came alive with green grass. The family all worked in setting out several long rows of strawberries, and they could scarcely wait until the green ones turned red. The weeds grew, well, like weeds, and almost every day Tim and Betty got in some exercise with their hoes and rakes.

Tim got to help his dad sow some lespedeza and timothy seed. After the fields were prepared for sowing, Mr. Smith and Tim would fill their seed bags, which fitted over their shoulder, and then with a sweeping motion, they would fling the seeds into the air. One by one they'd land on the fertile soil which had been plowed, disked, and harrowed. Horses loved timothy hay, and lespedeza was an inexpensive grass which grew well in that part of Missouri. In one field they planted soybeans, and in another alfalfa hay, which put nitrogen into the soil and was a hay rich in nutrition for the calves, which they were fattening to butcher. As the days lengthened and it became warmer, it was time to plant the corn crop.

"You know this farm work wouldn't be bad at all," Tim said to his dad, "if we weren't interrupted twice a day with those milking and feeding chores."

"Of course you're right, Tim, but those are the chores which are our bread and butter, and the crops make us a little bit extra. If the weather cooperates, that is."

"You know what, Dad? When Otto and I were fishing in our big pond the other day, Otto said we had some muskrats building their burrows in our pond bank. He said if we didn't get rid of them, they would completely drain our pond. He said females give birth to as many as three litters of three to eight young each year. He offered to help us trap them. He said their fur is sold as 'Hudson Seal' after it's been dyed and the longer hairs have been removed."

"Great idea. Tell him that he can keep all the furs he can trap as payment for getting them out. With 15 head of cows and several horses and mules, that water supply is essential for us to succeed at farming."

Tim called Otto that evening and told him what his dad had said. Otto set out several traps and the battle with the muskrats began.

Chapter 25—Pony Birthing

Dovie had been looking forward to the coming birth of her pony. Mr. and Mrs. Swartz let her take one of their mare ponies as a 4-H project for the year. She named her "Mummy" and they bred her with Lightning. Now almost eleven months had passed and when Dovie would see Betty at recess or lunch, she liked to discuss ponies, especially since Betty's horse, Blaze, was also due to give birth soon.

"Will there be any signs we can look for which will let us know when they are about ready to have their baby?" Dovie asked.

"Well, you've noticed how big they've gotten around the middle, I'm sure. Otto told me that sometimes when they are close, they'll lie down and after a while get back up several times during the day. And once they develop wax droplets on their teats, it means it's almost time."

"I'll let you know when that happens; I've even started dreaming about that new baby."

"Try to practice patience, Dovie; we don't want the foal to be born before it is fully developed. God's timing is always best."

"I guess so, but I wish Mummy would hurry up. I've been using a currycomb on her every evening which she really seems to like. I see that she gets plenty of hay and water and salt, and I even take a pitchfork and toss out the dirty straw and put fresh straw in her stall every evening. If she has this baby without us having to call the vet, I'll have a very successful project in 4-H this year. How's Blaze doing?"

"She doing fine, but Tim and Otto think your pony will be born before mine. I just hope they don't get caught outside in a storm or something."

"I check on Mummy bright and early each morning. Mom says I need to quit asking them if I can get up and go check on her and just wait until I hear the roosters crowing and then hop out of bed and check on her. I noticed just yesterday she laid down a lot more than usual. She always gets up though when I come home from school to check on her. Her appetite still seems to be pretty good and she doesn't seem to be grumpy. I'd think carrying around all that extra weight might make even a pony hard to get along with."

The next Saturday the 4-H Club members of the horse club met to discuss their projects. They met at the Swartz home. Mr. Brown and Otto were their leaders. Mr. Brown's son, Curley, rode up on a riding horse he was very proud of. Sally rode over on her pony. Betty and Tim came in a buggy pulled by Thunder. A couple of other kids came riding their ponies also. Mr. Brown called the meeting to order and he asked Otto to lead them in the 4-H Pledge. In unison they repeated these words:

> *I pledge*
> *My head to clearer thinking,*
> *My heart to greater loyalty,*
> *My hands to larger service, and*
> *My health to better living,*
> *For my club, my community and my country.*

Then Mr. Brown asked Dovie if she would like to show them her project.

"I sure would. Just follow me to the barn. Mummy has been expecting you."

Dovie had the stall spick and span and Mummy got to her feet when she heard them coming. Dovie explained to them what she had been feeding the mare and that she curried her regularly and that her due date was that very week. Mr. Brown inspected Mummy's teeth and hoofs, and everyone looked her all over. Several noticed that her teats appeared to be lactating some and they predicted that the foal could be born at any time. When they returned to the house, Mrs. Swartz had refreshments ready which they all enjoyed as they listened to each other report on their projects. They then played a couple of games of dominoes, talked about when and where they would meet next time, and went back home.

On the way home, Tim turned to Betty and predicted, "I think Mummy will have a baby pony by this time next week."

"You're probably right. She certainly looks ready!"

The next morning, Otto picked up Betty in his buggy and they headed for the Methodist Sunday school in Everett. Mr. and Mrs. Swartz hitched up their buggy and Dovie ran to the barn to make a last minute check on Mummy before getting into the buggy.

"How does she look? Mr. Swartz asked.

"She looks great! She'll probably have a pony sometime this week. I just feel it in my bones."

"I don't know how good an indicator your bones are, but it does look like it won't be long now."

When they returned from Sunday school and church, Dovie jumped out of the buggy and quickly ran to the barn. They heard her scream and at first they thought something terrible had happened. She came running out of the barn with tears of joy streaming down her cheeks.

"Mom, Dad, Mummy's a Mommy! Mummy's a Mommy! She just gave birth to Twinkle! Quick, come see!"

Mr. and Mrs. Swartz both ran as fast as they could to the barn and there they saw Mummy lying on the hay with a long legged black-and-white-spotted baby pony struggling to get to its feet. Mummy was getting to her feet and started licking her first born.

"Is it a male or female?" Mr. Swartz asked.

"I don't know," Dovie said, "I'm so excited I forgot to check."

"She's a female," said Mr. Swartz, "And a beautiful one at that."

Mrs. Swartz took some of the rags which had been left nearby and gave Dovie some so they could help dry Twinkle off. Mr. Smith removed the afterbirth from the stall. Dovie, with tears in her eyes could scarcely keep her emotions in check as she said, "Twinkle, you're really here. I thought you'd never get here. And

Mummy you just did everything right. I'm sorry I tried to rush you into this. You and God knew best and I'm happy for everybody."

By this time, Twinkle and Mummy were both on their feet and Twinkle was beginning to nurse like she had done it all her life, and although her legs were a little wobbly, she was learning fast how to control them. Just then, Otto and Betty appeared in the barn doorway and Dovie ran to Betty and gave her a big hug as she told them what had just happened. From then on, it was just like another member of the family had been added, and that was exactly what had occurred. As they went back to the house, Dovie said, "You all go ahead and eat. I'll be a little late. I must make some phone calls and share the good news before I'll be able to eat a bite!"

In a couple of weeks the same thing happened at the Smiths' home. Only this time it was Blaze and she gave birth to a healthy brown and white spotted male colt named Sparkle. Again, there was great rejoicing as the miracle of new life was shared with family and friends.

The birth of their two ponies is the end of one story but the miracle of birth and the lives of those who care for them multiplied many times is what make the world go round.

Chapter 26—New Life

After the camp meeting, Otto did some deep soul searching as he thought about his present and future life. He had been living for himself and planning what he was going to do some day when he became King of Amarugia. He had day dreamed a lot in the past, but since he had become a Christian he began to wonder if becoming King of Amarugia was something God wanted for him or if it was something he wanted for himself. For one thing, the present King was wealthy and strong, and it looked as if he would remain King for many years.

One afternoon while he and Tim were fishing, he said, "I've been thinking, and I see now that I'm not better than anyone else and God may have a better plan for my life than for me to become King of Amarugia. It's just like a big load being lifted off my shoulders. You know, I used to think I was 'Top dog,' but now I know I'm just like everybody else. All of us guys put on our overalls just one leg at a time."

"Yeah, I know what you mean. Usually I make up my mind about things and do them my way, and then ask God to approve what I've done. Our preacher and my Sunday school teacher, Mr. Johnson, say that each of us needs to pray first and find out what God's plan is for our lives from day to day. I like what he said, 'life by the yard is hard, but by the inch it's a cinch.'"

"That's a good way to look at it," Otto said. "I've been reading in my Bible about the time Jesus told Nicodemus that he must be born again if he wanted to see the Kingdom of God and to do this he must have a spiritual birth as well as a physical birth. I believe I received a spiritual birth when I told God in my prayer I was sorry for my sins and I put my trust in Jesus as my Savior and Lord." Tim replied, "Me too, and now I want to let others know

I'm a Christian. Do you know where it is in the Bible that it tells about the meaning of baptism?"

"I asked my Dad the very same question," Otto said, "And he said the sixth chapter of Romans is one place to find the answer. I read it and it tells how water baptism pictures a person dying to the old ways and when one is raised up out of the water, it pictures him or her putting on a new life. Do you understand what I'm trying to say?"

"Yep, and doesn't it also say baptism by immersion pictures Christ's death, burial, and resurrection when He paid the penalty for our sins?"

"You got it, and it also paints a picture of the time when we will die and be buried, and in the future we will be given a resurrected body in heaven."

"Being a Christian isn't sissy," Otto said. "It's really what causes the whole world to make sense to me."

Tim said, "Also I read about God's Spirit entering our life when we become a Christian. A question is asked, 'Do you not know that you are a temple of God, and that the Spirit of God dwells in you? If any man destroys the temple of God, God will destroy him, for the temple of God is holy ... and that is what you are.'"

"Wow! That's kind of scary," said Otto. "But you know what? If everybody paid attention to that, then there wouldn't be so much drinking, fighting, and killing. It seems like here in Amarugia there's a fight after the dance every Saturday night and somebody ends up getting hurt. Yep! Becoming a Christian doesn't mean we can't have any fun in life; it just means we'll have a lot more enjoyment when we take care of our bodies and our souls."

Just then Otto's cork went under and he jerked the pole to set the hook. "This looks like a good one," he said. As he pulled the fish onto the bank he said, "That channel cat must weigh about three pounds."

They realized it was time to go, so they gathered up their fishing lines and fish and headed for home.

As they rode to their homes, Otto said, "I hope you will pray for me as I seek God's will for my life, and also pray for my mom. She is not a Christian. Her Indian upbringing has led her to believe in the Great Spirit, but she doesn't understand why Jesus is important. She doesn't realize Jesus died on the cross for her sins, too. I overheard Dad talking to her about becoming a Christian but she said she wanted to see if it made any difference in my life before she decided what to do. Pray that she will be able to see the real difference in me. It's like the Bible says, 'The former things are passing away and all things are becoming new.' Well, I had better get on home. Tomorrow, I'm taking your sister to visit the Baptist church. See you there!"

On Sunday, Otto could hardly wait until he could hook Lightning to his buggy and ride over and pick Betty up for Sunday school and church. Otto's parents and Tim and his parents both hitched up their family buggies and rode the two miles to their churches at Everett. Tim knew Otto would be visiting more with Betty than him on Sundays, and that was O.K. because he would have time to visit with guys and gals his own age. He could find out what they had been doing during the week, and ask them about living the new Christian life.

A lady named Hanna taught Otto and Betty's Sunday school class at the Baptist church. It hadn't been all that long since she had been a teenager, so she made the lessons very interesting and personal. Her husband and their young child attended, too. Karl, Spring Bunny, and Dovie arrived at the Methodist church in their buggy. Dovie attended a class with her age group, while Mr. and Mrs. Swartz attended a class with other couples.

The sermon they heard was based on the life of Joseph and how he continued to follow God even though his brothers sold him into slavery. His faith in God helped him forgive his brothers, and through it all he was able to rescue the entire family from starvation, when, with the Lord's help, he was able to move them to Egypt.

On the way home from church, Spring Bunny asked Karl many questions about the Christian faith. He explained, "The

Lord is still active in the affairs of people. He didn't just create everything and then leave it to run down like a clock. Through His Holy Spirit, He works in our lives today."

"I think you are right," she replied, "In the Indian culture we worship the Great Spirit, but Christianity shows us a personal God who came to earth in the form of Jesus. His death and resurrection shows me how Jesus paid the price for sin, and I can have my sins forgiven by trusting in Him. I've noticed a definite change in Otto's life since he became a Christian. I don't know why I didn't realize sooner that God is interested in what we do with our lives. I agree with the Smiths when they said they'd been so interested in making a living that they almost forgot to make a life." She looked at her husband.

"You know Karl, I think I am ready to trust Christ as my Lord and Savior and join the Methodist church." Karl smiled as a great feeling of peace came over him. He reached over, put his arm around her; pulled her close to his side, and kissed her gently on the lips. Now that his wife and son were also a part of the family of God, it made him extremely happy.

Karl asked, "You know our Methodists church offers a choice as to how a new believer is baptized. Would you prefer to be immersed or sprinkled?"

"I want to be immersed just like you, Otto, and Tim were," she replied. She couldn't wait to tell Otto, Betty, and Tim she had repented of her sins and was trusting Jesus Christ as her Lord and Savior.

Dovie, who was sitting in the back seat of the buggy, asked, "Mommy, can I get in the water too when you get baptized?"

"It's more than just getting into the water, Honey. When you accept Jesus as your personal Savior and understand 'Why' we get in the water, then you will be ready to get baptized. You keep paying attention in Sunday school and church and keep reading your Bible and you will know when it's time for you to accept Jesus as your Savior. Then, it will be time to get baptized. Your daddy and I will try to answer any questions you may have about God and how He wants us to live."

On a mild day Mrs. Swartz joined two others in baptism at the Johnsons' pond near the church. She celebrated with her family at the Smith farm, where Betty and her mother had prepared a very special supper.

On the next Saturday when Otto and Tim were out riding, Otto said, "At our house, we have started reading a few Bible verses and have a prayer just before breakfast each morning. This morning we read in the book of James that if anyone lacks wisdom, let him ask of God and He will give it to him. I can always use more wisdom, especially as I look for what the Lord wants to do with my life."

Tim said, "When we lived with my grandparents, my grandmother used to have a list of subjects and we would choose a different one each day to look up in the Bible. I'm going to ask Mom and Dad if we can start doing that again. I learned a lot. I'm sure she still has that list and would give us a copy to use. I remember there was a good one about the armor a Christian should use. It said to have armor such as a helmet of salvation, a shield of faith, and the sword of the Spirit, which is the Word of God."

"Do you remember where that is found in the Bible?" asked Otto.

"I think it is chapter six of Ephesians," said Tim, "But I know how to find out for sure. My Bible has a concordance in the back where I can look up a key word and it will have the name of the book, chapter, and verse where it can be found."

"You know what," Tim said, "We could look up all kinds of answers to our questions if we had a big concordance. When I save up enough money, I am going to get one of my own."

"Talking about the Bible reminds me of a joke," said Tim. "You want to hear it?"

"Sure".

"A mother asked her six-year-old son what he learned in Sunday school. He told her, 'Today our teacher told us about one shack, two shacks, and a bungalow....'"

"Oh, I remember this one. That story is found in the book of Daniel and is about three guys named Shadrach, Meshach, and Abednego. They are the ones the Lord protected when they were thrown into the red-hot furnace.

Well, it's getting late. I had better head on back home. Bye, Tim, See you later, alligator."

Tim smiled and replied, "After while, crocodile."

SUMMARY

In this novel we have observed two families struggling to make a living in and adjacent to the little community known as Amarugia in the early 1900s. In their interaction with the soil, animals, and others, they came to realize the difference between making a living and making a life. With God as their heavenly Father and all other believers as brothers and sisters in Christ, they became good stewards of God's creation and of their mission to point others to Him.

EPILOGUE

J. Vivian Truman, brother of President Harry S. Truman, always said he was the only man who ever lived in Amarugia—because nobody else would admit living there. He operated the Dr. K.P. Jones farm of approximately 230 acres around 1913 or 1914. He lived there for one year and he vividly recalled being an Amarugian resident where the mud was so deep that a man could merely hold on to the back of a horse-drawn wagon and get it stuck.

David Wilson reigned as Amarugia's King from 1895 to 1913. In his book, *Tales of the Amarugia Highlands of Cass County Missouri*, Donald Lewis Osborn tells that, after his reign as King, David Wilson went to Platte County, Missouri, and was a successful real estate broker in Kansas City. He ended up in Lee's Summit, Missouri, where his house was sometimes raided for gambling, and his sister Minnie had to bail him out and otherwise loan him money to keep him solvent. When Minnie died, David gave up his house and land to the Oldhams of Oldham Sausage, so he was allowed to live with them until he died in 1933. He had already buried his wife, Fannie, so his own tombstone had an incomplete death date until David's great-nephew, Donald Read, had it completed and also added the inscription "King of Amarugia 1895-1913". Donald states that since 2001 he has taken upon himself the Title of King of Amarugia, since it had lain idle.

In 1983, the Missouri Conservation Department purchased 1,041 acres in the Amarugia Highlands and named it the Amarugia Highlands Conservation Area. This area contains grassland, wetlands (95 acres), forest/woodlands, cropland, and old fields. Among the facilities and features are: a boat ramp, fishing jetty, Amarugia Lake (55 acres), and permanent streams (South Grand

River and South Fork Creek). For more information, go to the internet and type in Amarugia Highlands Conservation Area.

Drexel, Missouri, has been known as one of the mule capitals of the world. Later, as tractors and other machinery came along, there was not as much demand for mules but there is still a great love for horses in the area. Today, near the Drexel, Missouri, area is a pony and horse farm named the "Amarugia Horse Farm." For further information, go to http://www.amarugiahorse.com/.

Today, some farming still takes place in Amarugia. The 80-acre farm where the author lived during the 1930s is completely farm land. The farm house, barn, sheds, wells, and ponds are all gone. When he visited in June of 2007, the farm had a beautiful 80-acre field of waist-high corn growing there. Several families in the area now raise cattle. Much of the area is pastureland, and much of Amarugia has become a bedroom community for those who work in Kansas City and other surrounding towns and cities.

The tombstone of David W. Wilson,
King of Amarugia from 1895 to 1913.

AMARUGIA HIGHLANDS CONSERVATION AREA

CASS COUNTY
1041 ACRES

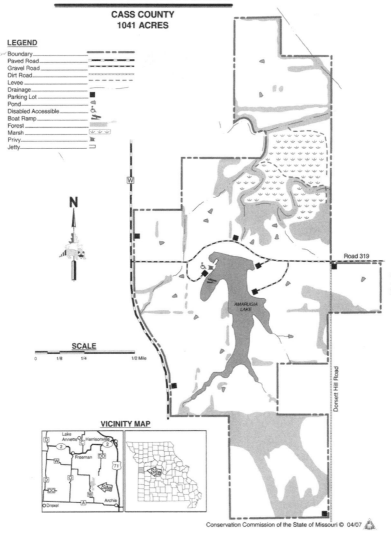

Missouri Department of Conservation Lands
Cass County

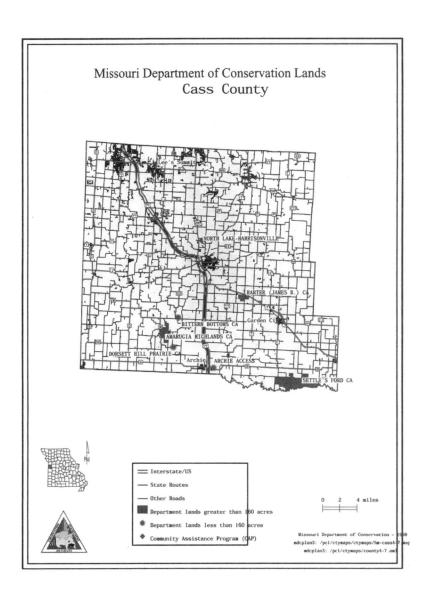

Interstate/US
State Routes
Other Roads
Department lands greater than 160 acres
Department lands less than 160 acres
Community Assistance Program (CAP)

0   2   4 miles

Missouri Department of Conservation - 1998
mdcplan3: /pc1/ctymaps/ctymaps/hm-cass4-7.map
mdcplan3: /pc1/ctymaps/county4-7.aml

THE BURNT DISTRICT MONUMENT

Only chimneys remained. They were call "Jennison's Tombstones" after the Kansas Jayhawk leader "Doc" Jennison, whose troops did much of the burning and looting.

In the Heart of the Burnt District
Harrisonville, Missouri

The Burnt District

Following the Civil War and the removal of civilians from Jackson, Cass, Bates and part of Vernon Counties as a result of Order No. 11 in 1863, those who returned saw a desolate landscape with only chimneys left to mark once flourishing farms and homesteads.

This monument commemorates the suffering which almost every family in western Missouri endured in the war years of 1861 to 1865 and the courage they displayed. Your generous donations will ensure that their stories will not be forgotten.

Our goal is $25,000. Cass County is donating the site, sidewalk and upkeep. Heartland Landscape is donating labor. Cass County Historical Society is raising the funds. Join us today!

The monument and memorial brick plaza will stand on the lawn of the Cass County Justice Center in Harrisonville, Missouri. Interpretive signs and plaques will tell the story of the Kansas Jayhawkers and Redlegs who plundered civilian businesses and farms and the guerillas who rose up to protect their way of life.

Looting and burning on both sides led Quantrill's guerillas to burn Lawrence, KS on Aug. 21, 1863 and execute over 150 men. In response, Union Gen. Thomas Ewing issued Order No. 11. All civilians in Jackson, Cass, Bates, and northern Vernon County had 15 days to leave. The countryside including all fields, homes, barns and goods were burned to establish a neutral zone where the guerillas could not hide.

The population of Cass County fell from 10,000 to 600. Only 30 percent of its residents returned after the war.

Those who returned started again, and the healing slowing began.

Donation Levels for
The Burnt District Monument

Commemorated on Plaques at the monument

- ❏ Platinum $5,000
- ❏ Gold $2,500
- ❏ Silver $1,000
- ❏ Bronze $500
- ❏ Friends $250

_____

Name

_____

Address

_____

_____

Phone

Memorial bricks will form a patio behind the chimney. Purchase a brick to commemorate an ancestor or family connected with the stories of the Civil War and/or show your support for the monument.

I wish to purchase _____ bricks @ $65 each

for a total of $_____

The bricks will be inscribed as follows (up to 4 lines with 15 characters per line)

Line 1 __ __ __ __ __ __ __ __ __ __ __ __ __ __ __
Line 2 __ __ __ __ __ __ __ __ __ __ __ __ __ __ __
Line 3 __ __ __ __ __ __ __ __ __ __ __ __ __ __ __
Line 4 __ __ __ __ __ __ __ __ __ __ __ __ __ __ __

Send your **tax-deductible contribution**
made payable to:

Cass County Historical Society, Inc. (a 501 c 3)
P.O. Box 406
Harrisonville, MO 64701

816.380.4396

cchs@iland.net

Robert L. "Bob" Gross visited the Amarugia Highlands
Conservation Area in the spring of 2007.

Author of **Amarugia** (Am-a-ROO-GEE)
Robert L. "Bob" Gross

He served as a Home Missionary of the
Southern Baptist Convention for 30 years (1961-1991).